P9-BEE-740

"You should not have chosen a mare, Beth, if you really wanted to win the race."

"You weren't riding a stallion this morning," she argued. "You—you deliberately tricked me."

"Dare I suggest that underneath you might not have been all that desperate to win? Maybe you like the fantasy of having a barbarian use you as his plaything!"

Beth was mortified to feel heat gather in her cheeks. Uzziah's smile was satanic. "You know, I think there is a lot more truth in that than you'll ever admit, my sweet savage. Perhaps it's up to me to discover just how much."

MIRANDA LEE is Australian, living near Sydney. Born and raised in the bush, she was boarding-school educated and briefly pursued a classical music career before moving to Sydney and embracing the world of computers. Happily married, with three daughters, she began writing when family commitments kept her at home She likes to create stories that are believable, modern, fast-paced and sexy. Her interests include reading meaty sagas, doing word puzzles, gambling and going to the movies.

Books by Miranda Lee

HARLEQUIN PRESENTS
1664—A DARING PROPOSITION
1702—KNIGHT TO THE RESCUE

Don't miss any of our special offers. Write to us at the following address for information on our newest releases.

Harlequin Reader Service
U.S.: 3010 Walden Ave., P.O. Box 1325, Buffalo, NY 14269
Canadian: P.O. Box 609, Fort Erie, Ont. L2A 5X3

Miranda LEE

BETH AND THE BARBARIAN

Harlequin Books

TORONTO • NEW YORK • LONDON
AMSTERDAM • PARIS • SYDNEY • HAMBURG
STOCKHOLM • ATHENS • TOKYO • MILAN
MADRID • WARSAW • BUDAPEST • AUCKLAND

If you purchased this book without a cover you should be aware
that this book is stolen property. It was reported as "unsold and
destroyed" to the publisher, and neither the author nor the publisher has received any payment for this "stripped book."

ISBN 0-373-11711-6

BETH AND THE BARBARIAN

Copyright © 1993 by Miranda Lee.

All rights reserved. Except for use in any review, the reproduction or
utilization of this work in whole or in part in any form by any electronic,
mechanical or other means, now known or hereafter invented, including
xerography, photocopying and recording, or in any information storage
or retrieval system, is forbidden without the written permission of the
publisher, Harlequin Enterprises Limited, 225 Duncan Mill Road,
Don Mills, Ontario, Canada M3B 3K9.

All characters in this book have no existence outside the imagination of
the author and have no relation whatsoever to anyone bearing the same
name or names. They are not even distantly inspired by any individual
known or unknown to the author, and all incidents are pure invention.

This edition published by arrangement with Harlequin Enterprises B.V.

® and TM are trademarks of the publisher. Trademarks indicated with
® are registered in the United States Patent and Trademark Office, the
Canadian Trade Marks Office and other in countries.

Printed in U.S.A.

CHAPTER ONE

'Is THAT the last one?' Beth asked with some dismay. 'They have no other stallions for sale?'

This was the third stud she'd visited, having spent all day yesterday at the huge Al Badeia farm just outside Cairo, and the day before at the nearby Government-run El Zahraa establishment, which boasted the most purely bred Arabian horses in the world. But not one had been able to show her a stallion that really caught her eye.

'I'm afraid so, *mademoiselle*,' returned the French bloodstock agent Beth had hired in Cairo. 'But I will ask again for you.'

He turned away to speak to the studmaster, who shot her a look that suggested he resented wasting time on so stubborn and stupid a woman. Though perhaps his attitude came from his cultural bias against doing business with a woman, Beth decided. *Any* woman.

She bristled and glared back at him quite boldly. The Egyptian's dark eyes flashed, his fleshy lips curling in open contempt. But at least he looked away.

Beth fumed in a barely held silence. She had no time for chauvinists. Actually, she had no time for most men. She had yet to meet one—other than Pete, of course—who treated her with the respect of a true equal. Even in her homeland of Australia, most of the males seemed to be blighted by the deeply ingrained belief that they were innately superior to the female gender.

Maybe that had validity back in the caveman days, she conceded, when a man's size and strength was necessary for survival, when the female species was forced to seek the physical protection of the male. But she couldn't see the worth of that argument in today's so-called civilised society.

Besides, at almost six feet tall and a muscle-toned one hundred and thirty pounds, Beth had the physical edge over most men she met. She could toss a bale of hay up on to the top of a pile without batting an eyelash, and when it came to controlling a feisty horse she was without peer.

But men didn't value such talents as throwing a bale of hay or controlling a difficult horse, she accepted with a mixture of cynicism and wry humour. All they wanted was a pretty little dolly-bird on their arms and in their beds. Or else—to use a horse analogy—a broodmare in their private stables.

Well, she was no pretty little dolly-bird, that was for sure. And, given her discovery a few years ago that sex held little attraction for her, she couldn't see herself taking on the role of broodmare, either.

So, at thirty years of age, she was still single. And single she was likely to remain, Beth decided quite happily. She didn't think she was missing out on much. Weren't her horses her children? Didn't they love her back as devotedly as she loved them? What need could a husband possibly fill in her life?

At last, Monsieur Renault turned away from the voluble Arab and led her slightly to one side. 'I'm sorry, Mademoiselle Carney, but there are no other stallions here within your price range. Won't you reconsider this one?'

He indicated the grey stallion who was tossing his proud head over the nearby railing.

Beth shrugged disconsolately. The horse just didn't have that special something she was looking for, and which she would recognise immediately she saw it.

Sliding her hands into the pockets of her loosely fitting khaki trousers, she opened her mouth to speak when a noise overhead distracted her. A black helicopter zoomed over quite low, its enormous rotor blades sending up a huge cloud of red dust around them. The studmaster called out something to them in Arabic and hurried off in the direction of the main stables.

'Must be an important client,' she muttered, trying to keep the sand out of her eyes, and thinking it was just as well she wasn't wearing eye make-up. Or *any* make-up for that matter. It all would have melted in this heat. February might still be winter in Egypt, but someone forgot to tell the sun.

'Would you mind if I left you for a short while, *mademoiselle*?' the Frenchman said. 'There is a horse about to be put on show that I would like to see.'

Beth frowned. 'If you tell me a horse has just arrived by helicopter I won't believe you. Not even an Arabian is *that* docile in temperament.'

Monsieur Renault laughed. 'No, no. The horse came by road earlier on. That was the owner arriving. He's a very wealthy, very eccentric horse-breeder, the son of an Arab sheikh.'

Beth pulled a face. 'Oh . . . another Arab.'

'Only half-Arab, actually. His mother was an English missionary.'

'An English missionary? That's an odd combination, surely?'

'Rumour says the lady in question was captured by a remote bedouin tribe and brought to their prince as a gift. He had no option but to accept her into his harem or cause a minor war. I gather she—er—didn't go willingly.'

'How disgusting!' Beth shook her head in disbelief that such things could still go on these days. But then she realised the offspring of this unspeakable act might be over half a century old, or even older. This all could have taken place way back in the twenties or thirties.

The Frenchman's smile was wry. 'I dare say the lady wasn't unwilling for long. She certainly didn't make any complaints to the British embassy when she was released a year later. After all, Arab princes are given lessons in lovemaking from the earliest days of puberty. They pride themselves on their expertise in the boudoir.'

'Huh!' Beth snorted. 'As if any of their poor terrified victims would dare make a word of criticism in those days anyway. She'd probably have had her tongue cut out in retaliation!'

'It wasn't such a long time ago. I gather the son is only in his thirties. But please, *mademoiselle*, I must go and see this horse perform.'

When he whirled away and began to stride up the path between the yards back towards the main stables, Beth dashed after him, her curiosity piqued. 'What do you mean, *perform*? What sort of horse is it?'

'Half Arabian, half racehorse. Apparently it can jump very well and is to be put through its paces in the show-ring for some prospective buyers, then offered for auction.'

Her heart leapt. Half Arabian, half thoroughbred. What an exciting combination! If the breeder had successfully blended the stamina and tractability of the former with the size and competitive spirit of the latter, he would have produced an animal simply *made* for the show-jumping arena.

Show-jumping was Beth's passion. But she'd never been able to afford to buy a horse that could do all she asked, a horse that could fulfil her lifetime dream of representing her country in international show-jumping events, maybe even the Olympics! That was why she was here, with her life's savings in her pocket, to buy into a blood-line which could produce that sort of horse. She had thought a pure Arabian was the answer, but the breeding mix Mr Renault had just told her about might prove a stunningly successful compromise.

'Is it a stallion?' she asked breathlessly.

The agent ground to a halt, dark brows pulling together over his small brown eyes. 'A colt ... yes,' he said slowly. 'But would you be interested in such a horse, *mademoiselle*? He is not pure Arabian.'

'So what? If he can jump, I'm interested. Besides, there's no harm in just looking, is there?'

The Frenchman smiled. 'You Australians are such optimists. Come along, then. I gather the owner is not a man to dilly-dally. He does not like to spend too much time outside his *domaine*.'

When he moved off at a fast pace Beth had no trouble keeping up. She had very long legs.

'And what is this eccentric breeder called?' she asked as they strode companionably along. 'Some impossibly long Arab name, I suppose. Sheikh el Bahdahrah of Bahdahrahdarah?'

The Frenchman laughed. 'No. He's known simply as Uzziah.'

'Uzziah,' she repeated, thinking it wasn't a bad name. It actually had a subtle strength about it.

'And where is this Uzziah's domain?'

'Somewhere along the West Coast of Morocco. I'm not sure where exactly. He guards his privacy like a demon. To be honest, I have never met the man before and am quite interested in seeing what he looks like. The word is he's a man among men.'

'I'm more interested in seeing what his *horse* looks like,' Beth said drily, thinking to herself that there wasn't a man alive who could do for her what a horse could. 'How much do you think this stallion might bring?' she added as an afterthought. There was no point in getting her hopes up if she couldn't afford the animal.

'I have no idea. This stud has never offered one of its stock for public sale before.'

'Perhaps the price of oil dropping means the sheikh's son is having a garage sale,' she retorted caustically, not at all impressed with oil-rich Arabs. Or oil-rich anybody else, for that matter. What did they do for their money? Nothing! Merely drilled a silly hole that just happened to tap into one of the earth's great natural resources. It was obscene to make money that easily. Simply obscene!

The fifty thousand dollars she had eventually accumulated to spend on her life's desire had been the result of fifteen years' fanatical savings, a steady amount put aside each week from hard work and careful budgeting. Even her trip to Egypt was the cheapest package tour she could find, whereas this sheikh's son flew in like a prince all because his father fluked pitching his tent over the right spot!

It just wasn't fair.

Beth pulled herself up short before she blew a gasket. No use getting herself all worked up over life's little injustices. If she couldn't afford the horse, then she couldn't afford it. Besides, she hadn't even seen it yet. For all she knew, it might be cow-hocked and knock-kneed, and with the temperament of a stubborn mule.

Monsieur Renault led her not up to the main stables, but down a side path to where a circular yard—as big as a show-ring—was set up ready with jumps. A group of perhaps twenty men were already seated in a small, covered stand that overlooked the ring. Some were in Arab-style dress. But most wore Western clothes. Expensive Savile Row suits, by the look of them.

One of the Arabs was dressed a little differently in a long, flowing white garment. A red brimless hat with a tassel hanging down the side sat on his dark head. A *fez*, she remembered reading somewhere, worn by men from Morocco.

Clearly, here was the eccentric Uzziah. Beth felt a vague sense of disappointment as her eyes skated over him. He seemed handsome enough, she supposed, in a swarthy-skinned, black-eyed Arab fashion. But nothing special. Short too, his shoulders lower than the men sitting on either side of him. So much for his being a man among men.

Another exaggerated male legend bites the dust, she thought dismissively, and swung her attention back to the ring—and the jumps that had been set up. Some of them were astonishingly high, others quite difficult in their spacing. There was a triple that would daunt the most experienced jumper, and a wall even *she* might tremble at. Not that she would ever admit to such a thing!

Apparently, the horse was really going to be put through the mill for its prospective buyers. Beth hoped the seller realised that a horse bred and trained at a secluded stud might perform well over jumps at home, but after the stress of a long journey, and in strange surroundings, its performance might leave a lot to be desired. Colts were particularly sensitive to a change of scene, she had found.

'Are you coming up into the stand to watch?' Mr Renault asked.

Beth hesitated. 'I—er—I'd rather stay here,' she told the Frenchman.

'You'll be hot out here in the sun.'

'I'm Australian. A bit of sun won't kill me, but you go ahead. I can see more from here.' Which she probably could. But the truth was she disliked the way Arab men sometimes looked at her, their dark gazes a mixture of derision and lust.

Beth found this latter response to her quite surprising. She had no illusions about her looks. She wasn't beautiful, or pretty. At best, she might be called handsome, with her strongly boned face and statuesque figure. But ever since she'd landed in Cairo, Arab eyes had followed her movements everywhere. She put it down to her fair hair and unusual height—both uncommon in Arab women. Even so, she was still submitted to some very perturbing looks which made her occasionally wish she were safely at home in Galston Gorge.

But if you were safely at home in Galston Gorge, a little voice piped up, you wouldn't have the chance of buying a potentially exciting animal!

Beth felt a surge of adrenalin. She couldn't wait for the young stallion to make its appearance, couldn't wait to see if it lived up to her high expectations. Moving forwards, she put a foot up on the bottom railing of the wooden fence, her hands gripping the top railing, blue eyes skirting the ring and its surrounds.

There was not a horse in sight!

Beth frowned. For a man who didn't like to dilly-dally, this Uzziah was certainly taking his time having the horse brought in, she thought impatiently.

A minute passed. Then two. Monsieur Renault had been right. The sun was darned hot. Beth's foot dropped from the railing. She shifted, then raised her other leg, bending her head forward and absently running a hand up the nape of her neck to make sure her long, thick hair was still secure in its tight knot.

An agitated neigh snapped Beth's eyes upwards, and all the breath left her body.

A horse, with a coat like black satin, was being brought into the ring, a horse the like of which Beth had never seen before. And would probably never see again!

'Oh, my God,' she murmured, shaking her head in awe. 'What I wouldn't give for such a horse!'

It side-stepped into the ring, snorting and tossing its elegant black head, sixteen hands of powerful equine bone and muscle that at the moment was bitterly resenting being restrained. A slender young lad was in the saddle, gripping the reins with thin, nervous hands. The colt was too much horse for the boy, Beth decided, especially under these difficult conditions. The agitated animal looked as if he might break away at any moment.

But then Beth noticed there was another person holding the horse. A man. Not a boy. His body was

obscured by the horse's neck and shoulders, but she
could see his adult male legs mixed in with the
prancing colt's own limbs. They were as long and ath-
letic-looking as the horse's, encased in fawn riding
breeches and knee-high black boots.

Suddenly, the colt swung round and the man came
into view, one of his hands firmly on the bridle, the
other grasping a thatch of black mane.

Beth gave a small gasp of surprise. Now *here* was
a man among men, she decided, her eyes travelling
quickly from the top of the groom's glossy black head
to the tips of his glossy black boots. But while she
could admire his impressive male form—which was
scandalously displayed in tight riding trousers and a
flowing black shirt, open to his waist—years of being
turned off the male gender in a sexual sense allowed
her to study him quite objectively, much as she would
a horse.

Actually, the horse next to him stirred her senses
far more than the man did. The horse, she coveted.
The man meant nothing to her personally. He was
merely a fine specimen of the male human animal.

His description ran through her head with a clini-
cally dispassionate interest. Approximately six feet six.
Two hundred pounds. Shoulders like axe handles. Flat
stomach. Narrow hips. Powerful thighs.

He wasn't an Arab, she deduced, despite his olive
complexion and jet-black hair. He was too tall. And
his face was all wrong to be Semitic. The nose was
long and sharp, rather than hawkish, the cheekbones
high and extravagantly sculptured, the mouth wide,
with thin, cruel lips. His face was strong rather than
handsome, and full of angles. A commanding face,
not easily forgotten.

The stallion did a three-hundred-and-sixty-degree turn, taking the man round with him. Beth added taut buttocks to her mental list of the man's physical assets, not to mention the most amazing hairstyle she had ever seen on a male. His black hair was not cut short at the back as she'd thought after viewing him front-on, but was quite long, pulled back and secured at the nape of his neck in a rough pony-tail, tied with a piece of plaited leather.

Beth tried to imagine her male acquaintances back home in Australia trying to get away with a hairdo like that. My God, they would be laughed at and teased quite mercilessly by their mates. Somehow, however, she couldn't envisage any man daring to laugh at this individual. Long hair or not, he exuded a formidable air that was almost frightening. Certainly, he was not a man to be toyed with, or taunted. Not that Beth had any plan to do either.

He began talking to the boy in the saddle, giving him orders in Arabic, his deeply set dark eyes flashing with a mixture of impatience and concern.

He had every right to be concerned, Beth believed. The young stallion was not in a good mood. He was pawing at the ground with his front feet, skittering around with his back, a rebellious glitter in his eye. His wide, Arabian nostrils were flared, his neck arched arrogantly, and he was frothing slightly at the mouth. Experience told Beth he would not jump well, especially in the hands of a slightly built boy with as much strength in his biceps as a willow sapling had in its spine.

She smiled to herself. Let him jump badly, she thought. His price will go down; then I might be able to afford to buy him.

For suddenly, Beth wanted that horse, wanted it with a wanting that seized her heart and stomach, twisting them both into tight knots of anxiety and excited anticipation. She held her breath when the horse was finally released, half of her willing the animal to show its magnificence in flight over the jumps, the other half hoping he would fail abysmally and so put her dearest desire within her grasp.

Immediately, it was obvious that the colt had no intention of jumping at all. Rearing high on its hind legs over and over, it finally crashed to the ground, then began to pig-root. As Beth had suspected, the lad was no match for the young stallion. Any moment he would be summarily dumped. When the groomsman raced forwards to grab the horse's reins, it skittered sideways, then took off for a hair-raising gallop around the outside of the ring, quickly approaching where Beth was leaning against the fence.

She could see the fear etched on the boy's face. No... more than fear. Panic and utter despair. The man was going off his brain in the background, shouting to the boy and the horse in Arabic. Beth got the impression that what he was yelling would transfer into four-letter words in English. She sensed that the lad would be on the receiving end of more than words when this incident was over.

'Barbarian,' she muttered.

Her decision to act was both automatic and foolhardy. She would save the boy and the day, not realising that in doing so she would lose her heart's desire.

Her fingers flashed out as the horse passed by, reefing the reins out of the rider's hands and looping them over a nearby fence-post. The colt's head snapped round when the leather suddenly ran out, whinnying its anger at its freedom being so abruptly terminated.

'Quickly,' she commanded the boy. 'Out of the saddle.'

He merely stared at her, his hollow chest heaving, full lips agape, eyes wide.

Beth decided he didn't know English. It would never have occurred to her that in this boy's land women did not order men around, even fourteen-year-old ones. Her immediate concern was the giant who was rapidly bearing down on them both with a face like thunder. Acting rather than thinking, she slipped through the fence, reached up and hauled the lad unceremoniously out of the saddle and on to the ground. Ignoring the shouts of the approaching groomsman, she vaulted into the saddle and unhooked the reins.

'And now, my stubborn beauty,' she whispered harshly in the horse's ear. 'Let's see what you can *really* do!' And, with a decisive tug on the bit in its mouth and a 'don't try anything if you know what's good for you' kick in its flanks, she wheeled the animal away from the fence and set it boldly for the first jump, which was thankfully in the opposite direction to the furious-faced groomsman.

As they approached the jump, there was a moment of indecision within the ton of horseflesh beneath her, a moment when, if he chose, the young stallion could have still relieved himself of his alien rider.

But only a moment.

Beth had an uncanny knack with horses, which defied description. It was a combination of a lot of things. Lack of fear. Skill. Practice. But mostly love...

Horses felt her love for them through her firm but gentle hands. And they responded accordingly.

'Up and over, my beauty,' she urged. 'Up and over!'

He cleared the bar easily, and Beth patted his neck, whispering the sort of sweet nothings in his ear that had soothed many a fractious competitor in the past as she approached the next jump. It wasn't the language that mattered, she knew. It was the tone that steadied the nerves, as well as the lack of tension in her own muscles. All animals responded to a confident but relaxed master.

Three more reasonably difficult jumps passed by without incident, till finally they were faced with the triple. Beth knew if she didn't set the horse right for the first, all would be lost.

She gulped down the thickening in her throat and let instinct take over, but as soon as they took off she knew her instinct had let her down. She was used to jumping on grass, and the sandy ground had deceived her perception of distance. She'd lifted the colt too early. He would fall short on the other side. His legs were too long to put in two strides before lifting for the second jump. If he took that extra step he would be too close. He would surely hit the bar. They might even fall.

A cry of dismay welled up inside her as they landed as short as she'd feared, but she choked it down and, gathering the reins tight, allowed the horse only the one stride before urging him to leap as he had never leapt before, to *not* take that disastrous extra step. She felt his muscles bunch beneath her, felt his big brave heart almost burst as he took flight. But he carried her safely over the second jump, and then the third.

Truly, this was a magnificent animal, she cried within her thudding heart. Magnificent!

But even as she grew aware of the crowd clapping in the stand, suddenly she knew he would never be hers. Fifty thousand would not buy this horse. It wouldn't even buy his tail.

Tears threatened, but she rapidly blinked them away. She still had a job to do. The wall remained, higher than any wall she had ever sent a horse over.

There was no fear in her heart, however, as she spurred the horse beneath her forward. He would sail over this last obstacle with ease, such was his power and courage, such was his jumping ability.

With ambivalent feelings, she tried to savour the experience, holding her disappointment at bay while imprinting on her memory how it felt as the mighty beast gathered himself in readiness, then soared skywards, the epitome of grace and control as he landed perfectly on the other side and trotted proudly past the applauding people.

Only one man among the onlookers was not applauding. And that was because he had remained frozen by the fence during the entire performance.

Never had Uzziah seen such a woman.

His breath had stuck in his throat when she'd unexpectedly catapulted into the saddle, his shock changing to a stunned awe at the way she'd quickly brought the rebellious colt under control. When it looked as if she might falter at the triple his heart had jumped into his mouth, but she'd come through splendidly. Why, she could ride almost as well as he could!

It wasn't till she had reined the horse safely in after jumping the wall that Uzziah moved, only to become hotly aware that his body was in a state of acute sexual arousal. It startled then puzzled him, for the woman was no great beauty. In fact, she was the direct opposite of the women he liked to bed.

Yet, as he stared at the fair-haired Amazon trotting his horse around the dusty ring, his dark gaze became riveted to the rhythmic rising and falling of her body, and suddenly Uzziah ached to have her astride *him*, not his horse, to have her ride *his* body to a sweat-glistened exhaustion, not that excuse for an Arabian he'd been forced to breed. So great was the pain of his need that it brought him to a quick decision.

With a curt order to the boy standing beside him, he strode quickly from the ring, beckoning to the Moroccan in the stand with an impatient wave.

The Arab hurried over, the tassel on his hat swinging wildly when he halted to bow low. 'Yes, master?'

'I want you to see to the sale of that infernal horse,' Uzziah pronounced brusquely, 'then extend an invitation to the woman to spend this coming weekend with me in Morocco.'

'The woman?' Omar's head snapped up, setting the tassel swinging once more. 'You mean...*that* woman?' He pointed to Beth, who was about to dismount on the far side of the ring.

'Of course I mean that woman. Do you see any other woman here?' Uzziah's dark eyes flashed impatiently. 'Don't you think she will come, Omar? Well, maybe she will and maybe she won't. But something tells me she will. She is wild, that one. And Western. Has there been a Western woman yet who's refused me? Now, is my pilot ready to take off?'

'Yes, master, but, but——'

'I will expect you by tomorrow evening,' came the sharp edict. 'Do not fail me, Omar. I must have that woman.'

Omar flushed as he glimpsed his master's mammoth discomfort. 'Yes indeed, master,' he agreed, and bowed low once more.

Uzziah snorted, and strode off, dust flying in the wake of his large black boots.

CHAPTER TWO

BETH swung her left leg over the colt's glistening shoulders and slid down to the ground near where the young Arab lad was hovering. The stunned expression on the boy's face was almost comical. Smiling, she handed the reins of the now docile animal over to him, then glanced around to see what the groomsman's reaction was now that she'd delivered the horse back safe and sound.

Beth was surprised to find he had disappeared. She had been half expecting him to tear strips off her for doing what she did. Where on earth had he got to?

Her eyes scanned the ring and the surrounds, quickly landing on the Moroccan-looking gentleman in the white robe and red hat, who had left the stand and was even now hurrying across the ring towards her, a dark frown on his swarthy-skinned face. Oh-oh, she thought. Mr Uzziah was clearly not happy by what had just happened.

Beth gnawed at her bottom lip as she accepted she had taken a great liberty in riding this man's horse without his permission. Hopefully, she could make him understand her intentions had all been good.

Her agitation increased as the man drew near, especially when his black eyes narrowed and started to run over her face and body in a very thorough scrutiny. But there was no lust in his gaze, only an odd degree of bewilderment. Perhaps he was wondering how a mere woman could have ridden with such strength and skill.

Beth leapt to her own defence before he could say a single word. 'I do apologise for taking matters into my own hands, Mr Uzziah,' she launched forth, 'but I could see your rider was in trouble and I was worried he and your horse might get hurt. I realise it was presumptuous of me to take over, but I acted on the spur of the moment and I trust you will forgive me.'

She smiled what she hoped was a soothing smile. 'After all . . . there was no harm done, was there? And I did show your horse to advantage. To be honest, I was hoping to buy the colt myself. I've been searching all the studs in Egypt for such a horse. Only I fear I don't have enough money to purchase your magnificent animal.'

Beth knew she was rattling on, but, encouraged by the Arab's considered silence, she kept going. 'My name is Beth Carney, *Miss* Beth Carney. I'm from Australia, where I own a small riding school, but I've always wanted to own or breed a superb jumper and once I saw your colt here, Mr Uzziah, I . . . I . . .'

Her voice trailed away when the Arab's frown deepened. It took several seconds for the penny to drop.

'Oh. Oh, I *see*!' she exclaimed. 'You don't speak English. Oh, how stupid of me! Look, I'll go get Monsieur Renault. He can——'

'I do speak English, Miss Carney,' the Arab returned in a surprisingly British accent. 'But I am not Sidi Uzziah. I am his humble servant, Omar.'

Beth stared as the man bowed low.

'You are? Then who . . . ?'

She groaned silently. Where were her *brains*? Clearly one of the taller men sitting next to this chap in the stand had been Uzziah, dressed in an ordinary suit. Hadn't Monsieur Renault told her he was half-English? She glanced over at the stand, but everyone there had moved around, some standing in groups, some having come down to lean on the fence and look more closely at the horse. She had no idea which one was this Uzziah fellow.

'My master has already left,' Omar informed her, on seeing her searching glances.

'Left?' A prickle ran up and down Beth's spine. Only one man had left. Surely he didn't mean that barbarian of a groomsman was actually the *owner*!

'Yes. Left.' Omar pointed towards the horizon where the black helicopter she'd seen earlier was fast becoming a mere speck.

Beth stared back at the Arab. 'Are you telling me that the—er—man who led the horse into the ring was Mr Uzziah? The . . . the big man with the huge shoulders and the . . . the . . .'

The Arab nodded, his smile turning smug at Beth's stuttering. 'My master is, indeed, a man among men.'

Her mouth dropped open, then snapped shut. She could hardly argue with that statement. This Uzziah was, indeed, a man among men. Size-wise. She doubted the same could be said for his character, since he clearly insisted this poor man address him as *master*. Where did he think he was living, the big oaf, in the Middle Ages? Didn't he know slavery had been abolished?

'My master wanted me to thank you for the service you did him in riding his horse so splendidly,' Omar went on in his best sucking-up voice. Not that he thought he really needed it. Sidi Uzziah had been right. As usual. The woman was clearly so impressed with him that she'd been rendered quite speechless.

Omar felt very confident now of succeeding in the task his master had entrusted to him. The woman's wanting to buy a horse was a fortuitous bonus, a cover behind which her acceptance of the invitation he was about to extend could be given a veneer of respectability. Omar's many dealings with Western women had taught him to appreciate a liberated woman's pride. She liked to think it was *her* decision whom she bedded, not the other way round. Still, Omar had no doubt that once he got the woman back to his master's home, Sidi Uzziah would have no trouble in persuading her to join him in the main bedchamber.

'My master also asked me to extend an invitation to you to spend the coming weekend at his home as his honoured guest. He wishes to thank you personally, and also to show you some more of his magnificent horses. Perhaps, since you do not think you can afford this colt, Miss Carney, another animal can be negotiated upon. There are many fine horses in my master's stables.'

Beth could hardly contain her excitement. Oh, she didn't gave a hoot about visiting this fellow's precious master. Any man who treated his employees like slaves left her cold. But if Uzziah's stud was full of horses like the one she'd ridden here today, she would be crazy to pass up the offer. She'd often heard that a grateful Arab was given to presenting gifts of great value. Who knew? Maybe he would give her a horse like that black colt. Or at least allow her to buy one for a lot less money.

'That is very kind of your master,' Beth said, picking her words carefully. If she wanted to secure an equine bargain she would have to avoid treading on any toes. From what she had seen, Uzziah's toes were very big indeed, as was his ego. Her instinctive antagonism towards him would have to remain well and truly hidden during her dealings with these people. 'I would like to come,' she explained, 'but I have to be back in Cairo for my flight home next Tuesday. Would I be able to get to Morocco and back by then? Today's almost gone and tomorrow's Friday.'

Omar beamed widely. So! The woman knew where his master lived. Clearly, she had asked after him, undoubtedly because she had been interested in meeting him all along. Uzziah's reputation as a lover had obviously preceded him. Success was definitely assured. 'I will arrange everything. You will be safely delivered to my master by tomorrow evening, then returned to Cairo by the time your flight is due on the Tuesday.'

Safely *delivered*? What a strange turn of phrase! The Arab made her sound like an express parcel.

'But first,' he added, 'I must see to the auctioning of my master's horse.'

'Gosh, yes. I'd almost forgotten about that.' As she'd forgotten about Monsieur Renault, though he seemed well occupied, talking to a group of people in the stand. Other bloodstock agents, probably. Or potential clients.

Left alone by Omar, Beth made her way over to the shade of the stand. Monsieur Renault immediately bustled over, raving about her magnificent riding and suggesting that she was brilliant enough to try for the next Olympic Games.

'I would like to,' she rejoined, 'but first, I need the right horse, like the one I've just ridden.'

Monsieur Renault frowned. 'I fear your display has put that animal beyond your reach, *mademoiselle*.'

'I fear you might be right,' was her sighing reply.

Any lingering hopes Beth had of securing the colt were dashed once the auction got under way. Bidding *started* at fifty thousand dollars and rapidly reached over twice that amount. When it was finally knocked down for nearly two hundred thousand, she was disappointed but not entirely discouraged. How could she be, when she had such an exciting second string to her bow?

'You don't seem as disappointed as I thought you would be,' the Frenchman observed.

Beth's smile widened. 'I have something to tell you, something quite incredible.'

Monsieur Renault listened in deep silence as she explained about the invitation from the colt's breeder.

'And you're going?' he asked, a frown forming on his face.

'Of course! Why ever not?'

'You do realise that this Uzziah is a bachelor.'

'So?'

'Well—er—it's just that . . . um . . .'

The sudden appearance of Omar by their side put a welcome end to the Frenchman's humming and hawing.

'Do excuse me, *monsieur*,' the Arab said with another unctuous bow. 'Time is of the essence, Miss Carney, if we are to arrive by tomorrow evening. My car awaits to escort you back to your hotel.'

'Oh, but I was going to travel back to Cairo with Monsieur Renault here.'

'I'm sure Monsieur Renault won't mind if you come with me,' Omar said smoothly. 'I have a telephone in my car from which we can begin to make arrangements straight away.'

Beth threw the Frenchman a beseeching look.

He frowned, not at her, but at Omar. 'I trust Mademoiselle Carney will be well looked after?'

The Moroccan looked affronted. 'Arab hospitality has always been second to none, *monsieur*. Miss Carney will be afforded every comfort and consideration.'

'I don't doubt it, but that doesn't guarantee that she——'

'Please, Monsieur Renault,' Beth broke in laughingly. 'I appreciate your concern, but I am thirty years old, and well able to take care of myself. I'm quite happy to accompany Omar and have no fears for my safety.'

Goodness! The way he was carrying on, anyone would think she was about to be swept up into a white slave trade racket. Or was he worried that she, like this Uzziah's unfortunate mother, was about to be imprisoned in a harem against her will?

The thought amused her tremendously. Maybe Monsieur Renault hadn't seen Uzziah earlier. One look at him would have assured the Frenchman that such a male would have ladies on tap. He wouldn't need to kidnap a very ordinary-looking, overly tall, sexually retarded female to slake his desires.

'Ready, Miss Carney?' Omar said, giving her a highly satisfied look.

'Ready, Omar. Goodbye, Monsieur Renault, and thank you for all your help.' She extended a hand for him to shake, but he declined, coming forward to kiss her on both cheeks in the French fashion.

'Be careful,' he whispered with the second kiss.

The husky warning sent a shiver rippling down her spine. But she quickly dismissed the Frenchman's concern as totally baseless. Perhaps he was used to dealing with less capable women, the fluffy little feminine type who always seemed to be running into trouble with men. If he'd seen her in action at the local pub at home where she and Pete had gone for a beer every Friday night, and where the occasional man had bothered her, he wouldn't be concerned for her welfare. Beth had a mean right hook, as well as a tongue that could cut a man down to size at fifty paces.

A wry smile pulled at her wide mouth. If Omar or Uzziah got out of line, they would darned well wish they hadn't, that was for sure.

'Come, Miss Carney,' Omar urged once Mr Renault moved off. 'We must hurry. Sidi Uzziah is expecting you for dinner tomorrow evening and I dare not disappoint him.'

Friday dawned hot, but enquiries at the hotel desk the evening before had informed Beth that the Atlantic coast of Morocco could be a lot cooler than Egypt, especially in the evenings. She was instructed to carry a coat of some kind, which could be worn or taken off where necessary.

Beth donned her classic white linen trouser suit whose blazer-style jacket had long sleeves, then teamed it with a red silk shirt with short sleeves. Her hair was once again put up, though this time in a looser, more feminine style. Make-up was still kept to a minimum.

A light dusting of powder plus a dash of her new red
stay-on lipstick. She wore white sandals and carried
a red leather pouch bag that matched her red luggage.
This entire ensemble—including the lipstick—had
been her only extravagances for her trip, bought to
be worn on the plane. The least she could do, she
thought, was depart and arrive in style.

Omar bustled into the hotel foyer right on time.
His remark on how 'nice' she looked carried enough
surprise to be mildly insulting, but Beth found
enormous reassurance in it. Maybe Monsieur
Renault's whispered warning had planted a small
worry in her mind that Omar or his master *might*
somehow fancy her.

But Omar's backhanded compliment revealed that
he hadn't been too physically impressed with her the
day before. No doubt neither had his master, or he
would have stayed around personally to invite her to
his home, not sent an impersonal emissary.

From that moment Beth really relaxed, determined
to enjoy her good fortune of a free weekend in
Morocco, whether she ended up with a horse or not.
Being transported to the airport in the same black
stretch limousine she'd ridden in the day before was
very easy to take, as was the first-class accommo-
dation in the jet carrying them from Cairo to
Casablanca.

She had a window seat and was all eyes as the plane
zoomed up into a clear blue sky, heading for its des-
tination. For ages she was content to stare downwards, fascinated by the contrasts of the land beneath
her: great expanses of hot, parched desert which every
now and then gave way to narrow belts of fertility.
These were usually marked by the presence of a small

river, or an oasis. After a long while the sand dunes were left behind and they were soaring over a rugged, snow-capped mountain range whose slopes were mostly covered with dense forests of tall trees.

'Tell me, Omar,' she asked when she finally grew tired of watching the scenery. 'How long have you worked for your—er—master?' Heavens, but that word stuck in her throat!

'I do not work for Sidi Uzziah,' came the solemn reply. 'I *live* for him.'

Beth was taken aback. 'You mean you *are* a slave?'

'No... I am his faithful servant. Sidi Uzziah saved my life once, and my honour many times. In return, I vowed to devote my life to his service.'

'He saved your life? How?'

Omar frowned. 'I'm sorry, Miss Carney, but I cannot tell you any more. My master would not approve of my telling personal things about him to a woman.'

Beth bristled. There she was, beginning to think this Uzziah might have some redeeming qualities, when it turned out he was an even bigger chauvinist than she'd originally thought. Clearly, his English half had been well and truly swallowed up by the Arab! Next thing she knew, she would be obliged to wear a veil in his presence!

Truly! The man was an anachronism in the world of today. Didn't he know that women were actually running the governments of several countries these days? Or didn't he care? Maybe that was why he secluded himself away in this private domain of his. So that he could ignore progress and live the life of a feudal lord.

Well, she had a little surprise for him. She wasn't going to kowtow to any man, not even an Arab sheikh's son who had the power to give her the horse of her dreams.

Of course, she wasn't going to be rude, either. That would be cutting off her nose to spite her face. No... She would be very polite, and hope to hell he didn't come out with any remarks that would make her bite before she could help herself. Beth's tolerance of patronising, condescending males was not extensive.

'How long before we get to Casablanca?' she asked Omar after they'd sat there in silence for some time.

'We should arrive in time for the midday meal.'

'And how far from there to your master's domain?'

'Another couple of hours by helicopter. We shall be there well before the sun sets.'

'And what should I call your master? Sidi Uzziah, as you do occasionally?'

'My master will want you to call him simply... Uzziah.'

No kidding, she thought with dry surprise. The wonders of the world will never cease!

Another half-hour passed. Beth was actually beginning to doze off in her seat when Omar spoke up.

'Look, Miss Carney! The Atlantic... and Casablanca...'

She blinked and looked down, her breath catching at the sight of the huge white and silver city sprawled out beneath her. It was awesome, but also quite foreign, as Cairo had been. All those flat-topped roofs, not to mention the many domed mosques with their slender, towering minarets spearing up into the sky.

The plane tilted its wings as it arced out over the ocean before swinging round to begin its final descent. Beth automatically held her breath till they were safely on the ground and taxiing across the runway. Peering through the window, she glimpsed a group of veiled women on a nearby rooftop, and suddenly she felt homesick for familiar people and places. She longed for the green grass of home, for the smell of horses and hay, longed to leap into a saddle and ride across some open fields, feel the wind in her hair.

'Omar,' she said quite abruptly.

'Yes, Miss Carney?'

'Do we have to stop over here for lunch? Can we go straight on to your master's place?'

Omar nodded gravely. 'Your wish is my command.'

Beth sighed and sank back into the seat.

Omar smiled to himself. It was gratifying that the woman was so anxious to see his master. Very gratifying indeed!

CHAPTER THREE

BETH and Omar had been in the air for just over an hour, the sleek black helicopter following the coastline south from Casablanca, when suddenly Beth shot forwards in her seat.

'My God, what's *that*?' she gasped, and pointed towards a huge structure that seemed to be growing out of the cliffs ahead.

'*That*,' Omar explained with great satisfaction, 'is my master's home.'

Beth's blue eyes widened. That was a *home*? That... that... fortress-looking thing?

She stared in silent awe as the helicopter flew closer. Gradually, Uzziah's residence assumed a less forbidding shape, with some Moorish domes coming into view. But the whole place was still surrounded by high stone walls that could only be described as battlements.

Beth frowned. 'It's really a castle, isn't it?'

'Indeed it is,' Omar agreed, and launched into an explanation of its history.

Built in the sixteenth century by a rogue Moorish pirate, the castle commanded a small bay and estuary from which its daring owner had launched ships to loot the merchant galleons that strayed too close to the Atlantic coast. Positioned high on a strategic promontory, the citadel's carefully placed cannons had made short work of any battleships sent by the British and Portuguese navies, while the pirate's own small ships were safely hidden upstream in the narrow river.

As the helicopter drew even closer Beth could actually see the embrasures in the walls where the cannons would have been placed. How fascinating! Pete was not going to believe a word of this. Beth wished she had a camera with her.

Suddenly, the helicopter lifted high up over the battlements and domes, and once again Beth gasped. For right in the middle of the formidable structure was an ampitheatre of a courtyard into which the helicopter was very quickly descending.

Her eyes were everywhere, taking in the multi-storeyed verandas that surrounded the circular courtyard, the Moorish arches looking like gaping toothless mouths in the stark, whitewashed walls. Countless stone steps rose on all sides to meet the first of the verandas, and on these steps sat rows and rows of earthen pots full of pink and white geraniums.

The helicopter was by now hovering just above the courtyard floor, which Beth noticed was cobble-stoned. Maybe that was why the pilot was taking his time in actually landing, because the ground wasn't perfectly level. Finally, she felt a small shudder and shake and the rotors were out. They were down. She exhaled quite a large sigh, only then aware of the tension accompanying such a hair-raising descent.

'My master will come to meet you personally, Miss Carney,' Omar said as they both unbuckled their seatbelts. 'You go on ahead with him and I will take your luggage to your quarters.'

'Please don't feel you have to wait on me, Omar,' she said briskly. 'I'm quite capable of carrying my own luggage, you know.'

Omar's smile was wry. 'I'm sure you are, Miss Carney. But you know the saying. When in Rome, do as the Romans do. You are in Morocco now. Please . . . while you are here . . . try to put aside your liberated Western views and allow us to spoil you a little. It is expected.'

Beth sighed. 'Very well, Omar. But only because I don't want you getting into trouble. I'm not used to this type of thing. Back home, I——'

'Aah, but you're not back home, are you, Miss Carney?' he cut in smoothly.

She glanced out of the window at the alien scene before her eyes and nodded slowly. 'You're so right, Omar. So r . . .' Her voice broke off as an even more alien scene met her eyes. The man who had led the colt into the ring the previous day was making his way down the multitudinous steps towards the helicopter, dressed in the most exotic regalia she had ever seen outside a fancy dress ball.

'Heavens to Betsy!' she said breathlessly, her eyes almost popping out of her head as they raked over her host and his incredible clothes. He looked like something off the set of an Arabian Nights movie!

'Come, Miss Carney,' Omar urged. 'My master does not like to be kept waiting.'

Beth rose from the seat, still shaking her head. Now *this* Pete definitely would *not* believe!

The side door of the helicopter was slid back, letting in a gust of fresh air. With her red bag slung over her shoulder, she moved into the opened doorway, only to find herself looking down into the most striking pair of black eyes she had ever seen. Not to mention the most striking face.

Back in Egypt she had gained the impression that Uzziah wasn't handsome. Maybe he wasn't in a classical way. But my goodness, up close one could bear looking at those strongly sculptured features for some considerable time.

'Greetings, Miss Carney,' he said in a rich, cultured voice that would have done Prince Charles proud. 'Welcome to my home.' And, reaching up, he slid large hands under her armpits and lifted her down on to the cobblestones as if she were a featherweight.

Beth felt flustered for a second. Never had a man been able to make her feel so tiny and feminine as this one had just done.

Still, she reasoned, regathering her composure after feeling something akin to panic, she had known he was Hercules reincarnated, hadn't she? He even looked a bit like Hercules, garbed in those amazing clothes!

Disbelieving blue eyes swept down over them once more.

How come he didn't look ridiculous dressed in those black silk pantaloons and that ornately braided black leather bolero? He should at least have looked vaguely effeminate, especially with that flashy purple cummerbund around his waist and his hair slicked back in the same outrageous pony-tail he had sported the other day.

Instead, Beth had to confess that Uzziah looked more male than any man she'd ever clapped eyes upon, his scantily clad chest drawing a reluctantly admiring gaze. Incredible muscles bulged all over his bare arms and his smooth semi-naked torso, his skin carrying a sheen that bespoke having been massaged with some kind of oil.

No sooner had this thought insinuated than the aroma of sandalwood drifted up into Beth's nostrils. She breathed in, appreciating the heady scent for a few unguarded moments, as she was appreciating Uzziah's magnificent body.

Good grief, what am I *doing*? she berated herself. The man will start thinking I fancy him if I keep this up.

Impossible to explain that she would be similarly impressed by the body composition of a fine stallion, and that her blatant staring had nothing to do with his attractions as a member of the opposite sex. Why, the last man on earth she would ever be attracted to was a man who allowed another human being to call him *master*!

Still annoyed with herself for gawping like an adolescent schoolgirl, Beth quickly pulled herself together, squaring her shoulders and standing up as tall as she could. Unfortunately this still fell several inches short of her host's massive stature, forcing her to crick her neck back to look up at him.

'It was so kind of you to invite me for the weekend,' she said with cool politeness.

Her host stared down at her for a moment, making Beth worry that she might have put too much starch in her voice. She didn't want to offend the man. Her intention was merely to correct any false impression her staring might have given him. Suddenly, her hope of securing a free or cheap horse began to fade. Desperate, she dredged up a smile, relieved when her host smiled in return.

'Aah ... But it was *more* than kind of you to save my reputation as a breeder of impeccably behaved horses,' he said, startling her again with that posh English accent of his.

Goodness, but he must have spent some considerable time within the hallowed walls of a toffy British school to acquire such a voice, Beth decided. He certainly hadn't been educated in the desert sands of Arabia, that was for sure. Or Morocco, for that matter.

'I will be eternally grateful,' he finished with a gallant little bow.

That's not necessary, was her rueful thought. Just give me one of those impeccably behaved horses and we'll be all square in the eyes of Allah.

'I trust Omar has looked after you well?' he continued.

'He's been very kind. And do call me Beth,' she finished with another polite smile. Nobody could say she wasn't giving this her best shot.

'My pleasure...'

'Omar says I'm to call you Uzziah. Is that all right?'

'I wouldn't have it any other way. Come... let us go inside for some tea. Omar tells me you refused refreshments at Casablanca. He said you were most anxious to come straight on here.'

Beth shot a frowning glance over her shoulder in Omar's direction but he was busy attending to her luggage and was not looking her way. Clearly he had telephoned from Casablanca airport, which was only reasonable, but she wished he hadn't made it sound as if she was some silly woman panting to be in this man's company.

Not that that would be an unusual occurrence, she conceded drily to herself. A lot of women would probably find this Uzziah's macho looks very sexy.

He was also demonstrating a civilised charm today that had eluded him back in Egypt.

Maybe he donned the silken voice and manners along with the silk trousers, she thought cynically, for nothing would ever eradicate her first impression that he was a barbarian at heart. Beth strongly suspected that beneath this deceptively sophisticated façade lay a far more primitive individual, a man who did not always follow society's rules.

Monsieur Renault's whispered warning filtered into a corner of her mind. Perhaps her host had a reputation as a ladies' man. Beth didn't seriously think *she* was the object of any sexual intentions on his part but, just to be on the safe side, she resolved not to smile at him too much.

'Tea sounds excellent,' she said crisply.

'Shall we go inside, then?' Uzziah suggested, and curved a hand around her left elbow.

Beth knew it was a normal gentlemanly gesture to take a lady's arm, especially when going up a flight of stairs. Yet as Uzziah guided her up the many steps, his large palm firmly around her flesh, she felt vaguely disquieted and once they reached the veranda she quickly jumped on any excuse to ease away from his touch.

'My goodness, I've never seen such a beautiful floor!' she exclaimed, and bent down to look more closely at the mosaics that covered the veranda. They were, indeed, beautiful, made up of small squares of marble tile in many different shades of blue, all intricately placed to form startling geometric designs.

'You will find many marvellous examples of Moorish art and architecture here to admire,' her host remarked. 'Tomorrow I will give you a more extensive tour. But for now, I think some afternoon tea, then a small siesta before dinner is called for. Flying can be quite exhausting.'

Beth did actually feel quite tired now that her feet were solidly on the ground. Her earlier desire for a ride had well and truly dissipated. Maybe in the morning...

'I think you could be right,' she said, stifling a yawn.

'Come, then...'

This time, he didn't attempt to take her elbow and she accompanied him in a much more relaxed state. Soon they had left the shaded veranda to move along a massive high-ceilinged hallway that was as wide as a room and as rich-looking as the interior of a French château. A Persian carpet in vivid colours softened their tread on the black marble floor and huge bronze filigree lanterns lit their way.

Beth cast brief glances at the amazing and highly erotic murals that adorned the walls on either side. She rolled her eyes at the excessive nudity, not to mention the rather extraordinary positions and activities several of the naked bodies were engaged in. She supposed some people might have found such depictions fascinatingly interesting. For her part, Beth found them simply tedious.

As Pete always said about X-rated movies: if you've seen one, you've seen them all! Besides, she was quite sure the artists had exaggerated certain areas of the male anatomy. Typical! Everything about sex was an exaggeration, in her opinion. Men talked big but, when it came right down to it, the reality was a very small experience.

'You don't approve of nudity in paintings?' Uzziah remarked as they walked under another of the intricately carved arches that spanned the corridor at regular intervals.

Beth darted a sidewards glance at her host who was watching her intently. Darn! The last thing she wanted to do was insult the man's sense of artistic taste. Clearly he liked these paintings, otherwise they wouldn't be all over his walls. Yet there she'd been, turning her nose up at them.

'Oh, no, I like it,' she lied outrageously. 'Nudity is very—er—natural, don't you think?'

Uzziah's mouth creased back into a slow smile. 'My feelings exactly. The world is far too full of hang-ups where sex is concerned.'

Beth blinked. *Sex*? She thought they were only discussing nudity.

Fortunately, the arrival of a pair of heavy wooden doors in their path terminated that topic. And not before time too, she considered. She hated talking about sex.

Uzziah reached out to grip the two bronze knobs, turning them and throwing the doors wide open. Beth tried not to gape.

The room beyond was as large as the largest ballroom. Great expanses of cool, uncluttered space stretched before her, a shiny white marbled floor underfoot and a highly ornate ceiling overhead, from which hung several enormous crystal chandeliers. Plaster friezes covered the walls, against which tall earthen pots stood at intervals like silent sentinels. Halfway across the room the floor was raised like a platform, with several steps leading up to it.

And that was where the furniture was placed. Low divans made in rich velvets and covered with plump cushions grouped around equally low tables carved in dark wood, all sitting on the most highly exotic patterned carpet. Behind the seating arrangement, the room stretched into a large, semicircular alcove, where the curved glass windows were covered by an intricate black fantasy in wrought iron. One could just glimpse the darkening sky through the gaps in the iron arabesques. It looked cold and forbidding, with banks of clouds blocking out the setting sun.

Inside the castle it was anything but cool, however. Beth suspected the whole place was air-conditioned. She had spotted the cleverly concealed vents in the walls and ceilings.

The man had to be a multi-millionaire to afford all this, she decided, though without any admiration. No doubt his father had provided all. Uzziah had only needed to withdraw from his daddy's gushing bank accounts to buy whatever he wanted, from historical castles to pedigreed horses.

Her one consolation when thinking about such an irritating situation was that there were some things money could not buy. Such as love and respect. But maybe this Uzziah didn't want or need either of those things. Maybe he survived quite well on the substitutes of sex and slaves.

'You are frowning again,' Uzziah remarked. 'Most women find my private quarters very pleasing to the eye.'

Beth gathered herself once more, finding another soothing smile. 'And they are,' she said quite truthfully. 'Exceptionally so. But I just remembered I left my camera back in the hotel in Cairo. I would dearly have liked to take some photographs to show my friends back home.' Brother, this lying was getting to be a habit. Not only that, she was getting darned good at it.

Or was she?

Didn't her host's left eyebrow lift a little just now?

'Is that all?' he said silkily. 'I'm sure Omar will be able to find one for you to borrow during your stay.' With that, he stepped over to one side of the open doors and pulled a gold sash that was hanging from the ceiling.

It wasn't Omar who answered Uzziah's summons, however, but a ravishingly beautiful young woman with long black hair and skin like toasted almonds. Surprisingly unveiled, she was dressed in a flowing floral skirt and an embroidered white blouse. Several gold necklaces hung around her neck, large gold hoops dangling from her ears, giving her a Spanish rather than Moroccan look. She must have anticipated her master's wanting tea, for she came in carrying a tray already prepared. No ordinary tea tray and service either. It looked like solid silver and must have cost a king's ransom.

The girl slanted Beth a shy smile as she entered, bowing slightly to Uzziah before moving gracefully across the marble floor and up the steps where she placed the tray on the low table.

'That will be all for now, Aisha,' Uzziah commanded. 'But I wish to see you later...'

'*Oui, monsieur,*' the girl answered in French, though it was obvious she had understood his English. It was also obvious she knew why Uzziah wanted to see her later, for she flushed prettily and kept her lashes lowered as she left.

Beth was also *au fait* with her host's intentions, since Uzziah had not bothered to hide his lust for the girl. His penetrating black gaze had followed her every movement from the moment she'd entered the room, devouring her full, unfettered breasts as they moved beneath the thin cotton blouse. Even now, as she was closing the doors, he kept staring after her, an intense expression on his face.

Beth found it hard to hide her disgust. Maybe the girl was willing. But maybe she wasn't. Somehow Beth didn't think Aisha's feelings would be consulted.

Still, she could not afford to sit in judgement of her host's decadence or it was sure to show in her face. Clenching her teeth hard in her jaw, she assumed an inoffensively bland expression just as Uzziah's gaze moved from the departing girl to herself.

For a moment Beth could have sworn it was *her* he was looking at with desire. But logic reasoned that the hungry glittering in those ebony eyes *had* to be the leftover effect of the voluptuous Aisha's visit, a conclusion reinforced when Uzziah's face swiftly assumed a frown that betrayed a degree of irritation. Or was it frustration?

'Come, my dear lady,' he said almost brusquely. 'Our tea awaits...'

CHAPTER FOUR

BETH quickly realised that afternoon tea was not going to be the teabag-in-the-cup variety, with a couple of plain bisuits in a saucer. The tray Aisha had left contained a teapot, a large lidded jug, three matching silver canisters, two dainty glass mugs, a plate full of cakes and another of fresh fruit.

After she'd settled herself down on to one of the softly cushioned divans, Beth watched with a degree of curiosity as her host began doing the honours of making the tea himself. This surprised her. She would have thought he'd have had the girl stay and do it.

Somehow, the serving of tea didn't fit her mental image of Omar's master. Yet clearly he had done it many times, for he was neither hesitant nor clumsy. With deft movements, he took the lids off the three silver canisters and began spooning from each one into the teapot. First came tea, then mint leaves, then rough cubes of sugar—*many* cubes of sugar—then more tea, mint and even *more* sugar.

Beth, who took her tea black and unsweetened, opened her mouth to protest but quickly closed it again. Instinct warned her that this was some sort of ritual, this serving of mint tea. If she said anything, she might risk offending the man again. So the drink was going to be overly sweet. So what? She could surely stand it for a day or two if it meant keeping on the right side of her host.

Finally, steaming water was added and a strong, minty aroma filled the air.

'Have you had mint tea before?' Uzziah asked, glancing down at her from his enormous height.

'No,' she admitted, wishing he would sit down. Her neck was beginning to ache from looking up at him.

'You'll like it. Women always do.' Suddenly, he did sit down. But not quite the way Beth had anticipated. Sweeping a huge cushion from a nearby divan, he tossed it down on the floor near her feet, then sank down upon it, yoga style. This put his piercing dark eyes on a level with hers and his scantily clothed body very close.

Beth found his nearness quite disturbing. She liked her personal space and felt almost claustrophobic with him sitting in front of her like that. The thought that she couldn't move away from him, even if she wanted to, rattled her slightly. But she had no option, in the circumstances, than to hide her fluster and accept one of the cakes from the plate he was offering.

If I don't get a darned good horse out of this, she grumbled to herself, I'll just spit!

'You will like these also,' Uzziah said in his cultured English voice.

Don't be too sure of that, she thought drily, never at her best when men presumed to tell her what she would and would not like. Beth hadn't let a cake pass her lips in years, her once sweet tooth a thing of the past.

But good manners insisted she take at least one cake, and she selected the smallest. 'Thank you,' she said politely, and took a tiny bite from the foreign-looking food, wondering if swallowing it was going to be as difficult an experience as she feared drinking the tea would be.

But the cake wasn't overly sweet, its flavour one of spice and almonds. 'Mmmm,' she murmured, not without surprise. 'You're right. I do like it.'

'Did you doubt me?'

His smile carried a sardonic edge which puzzled Beth. Truly, he was an enigmatic man. A man of mystery.

For the first time since meeting him, she thought about his unusual background. She could see both the English and the Arab in him. Which parent, she wondered, had actually brought him up? Or had both had a hand in forming this strange mixture of savage and sophisticate?

Naturally, she dared not ask such personal questions. Omar had given her fair warning. Uzziah liked his privacy.

'Morocco prides itself on its cakes and pastries,' her host informed her, and turned away to start pouring the tea into the glass mugs with the silver handles.

This put some welcome space between his semi-naked chest and her knees.

'And on its Arabian horses too, I would imagine,' she added, deciding to bring the conversation round to a safe topic. Not to mention the main purpose of her visit.

He darted a sidewards glance at her from under his dark brows. 'Yes, of course. The Arabian horse as it is known today was bred here in the Barbary States of North Africa at least a thousand years before it was bred in Arabia. So it is, in fact, more Moroccan than Arabian.'

'Truly? I didn't know that. I always thought they were originally bred in Arabia by the bedouin tribes.'

'They would like to think so, but no... that was not the case.' He handed Beth a mug of the highly aromatic tea, then picked up his own. 'So... You like Arabian horses, do you? Omar tells me you were in Egypt hoping to purchase a stallion for your stud back in Australia.'

Beth laughed, which brought a swift frown from her host.

'Please don't be offended...' She gave another chuckle of amusement. 'It was just that it was funny hearing my little establishment called a stud. It's only a small riding school with not an Arabian horse in sight, I'm sorry to say.'

'Really?' He took a sip of his tea, his black eyes studying her over the rim of the cup. By the time the cup left his mouth a deeper frown was creasing his high, wide forehead. 'Why do you wish to buy an Arabian stallion, then? Why not an Australian-bred one?'

'I've always adored showjumping,' she explained. 'I ride in top shows for a wealthy neighbour of mine. Only his second-string animals, of course. But I noticed his best horses always have Arabian blood in them. I've been saving my money all my life to buy an Arabian colt who can jump well, one everyone at home will envy.'

'Especially this—er—wealthy neighbour?'

Beth was amazed to find herself colouring guiltily under her host's knowing glance. Surely he couldn't have guessed about Vernon, could he? No, no, he couldn't have.

'Maybe,' she returned with admirable nonchalance.

Yet inside, the old bitterness—and regrets—welled up again. How *could* she have gone to bed with Vernon, after all she knew about him? The man had seduced practically every available female in the horsey set around Sydney. And boasted the fact! Her own capitulation proved how easily a woman's head could be turned by a handsome face and some flattery, especially when that woman had for so many years received nothing from men except insults about her appearance.

Beth knew full well that if she had not lost all that weight back then Vernon would never have looked at her twice. But five years ago Pete had discovered he had a cholesterol problem and their meals had undergone a drastic change. And so, subsequently, had she! The extra pounds she had always carried had dropped off her. She had suddenly shown up at the annual showjumping ball, unexpectedly slimmer and done up to the nines. Dear old Vernon had taken one look at his revamped neighbour and automatically gone into top seduction gear.

What still irked Beth was that she had allowed herself to be seduced, like so many women before her. Hell, she hadn't even got any pleasure out of it! Not even a *hint* of pleasure. Since Vernon's reputation as a lover was second to none, Beth had been left with the unfortunate conclusion she was a complete flop where sex was concerned. Still, by then, she had already decided she didn't like men much anyway, especially rich ones!

The only way she'd been able to salvage her pride afterwards was to go on riding Vernon's horses as though nothing had happened between them.

Vernon—the rat!—had been only too happy to return to their previous status quo.

Beth was still fuming inside over the likes of Vernon Van Horn when she put the cup of mint tea to her lips and sipped, forgetting that she wasn't supposed to like it. So the discovery that she did startled her. 'Oh! This is really nice too,' she said with more surprise in her voice.

'Well, of course it is,' her host pronounced, an amused twinkle in his eye. 'Didn't I say you would like it? You'll have to learn to trust my judgement while you're here, my dear Beth. I dare say there will be a lot of new experiences for your tastebuds over the coming weekend.'

'Yes, yes, I suppose so,' she said politely, vowing to make a valiant attempt to eat whatever was set before her—however weird—if it meant going back to Australia with a horse like that black colt.

Thinking about the colt quickly returned Beth's attention to her host, who was still watching her over the rim of his cup. Pasting a smile on her face, she lifted her own cup to her lips and began to sip.

'When you've finished your tea,' Uzziah said, 'you must tell me how you learnt to ride so brilliantly. I confess I have never seen a horsewoman of your strength and skill. We must go riding together tomorrow.'

Beth's smile was genuine this time. 'Oh, I'd adore that. I was thinking earlier today how much I've missed my horses. And riding . . .' Her sigh of longing was deep.

'There is no need for you to be missing any of your pleasures while you are here, dear lady,' Uzziah said in his deep, rich voice. 'It will please me to gratify your every wish during your stay.'

A prickle of excitement rippled up and down Beth's spine. Things were going very well, very well indeed!

'You're most kind,' she murmured.

Her host startled her with a dry laugh. 'So I've been told. Occasionally. My motives are invariably misunderstood. My mother tells me I'm the most selfish man in the entire world.'

Beth was taken aback by this mention of his mother. After Omar's warning, she had not expected Uzziah to make any personal remarks. Still, she was not about to waste the opportunity to satisfy a little of her curiosity concerning this enigmatic man.

'Does your mother live with you?' came her innocent-sounding query.

Unfortunately, it brought a very curt, 'No.'

Beth fell silent, since to pursue that line would have taken a hide as thick as an elephant's. While she could be blunt on occasion if provoked, she was never deliberately rude.

'My mother is a typically interfering parent,' her host pronounced at last in an irritated tone.

Beth said nothing, though his comment rankled. Didn't he know how lucky he was to have a mother alive and well? Hers had died from cancer many years ago and she still felt the loss.

'Let us not speak of mothers,' Uzziah growled. 'Horses are much more amenable creatures. Tell me, Beth, how young were you when you rode your first horse?'

'I have no idea,' she shrugged. 'I've been riding as long as I can remember. Two, I suppose. Or maybe three.'

'As I suspected . . . Riding is as natural to you as walking.'

'More like breathing,' she said with a rush of fierce emotion. 'I *live* for my horses. Without them, I would surely die.' Suddenly, the thought of life actually *without* her horses sent a strangling lump into her throat. 'I'm sorry,' she choked out, swallowing convulsively. 'I'm being fanciful.'

He stared at her for a moment then slowly shook his head. 'No . . . I don't think so. I have often felt the same. They get in your blood, horses. One can certainly live and breathe them. I sometimes think I would rather possess a fine horse than a woman!'

Beth tried not to show shock at this turn of phrase, though it was not so different from her own view. Weren't her horses a substitute for marriage and a family?

Holding his flashing black eyes with a steady gaze, she replied coolly. 'I can't say I have ever thought to make such a comparison.'

His laughter carried dry amusement. 'I certainly hope not. Here . . . try a different cake and some more tea. Shortly, I'll show you to your quarters where you can rest for a couple of hours. Dinner will be at eight.'

Once again Beth had to bite her tongue to stop a protest from escaping. Omar's words loomed large in her mind. When in Rome, do as the Romans do . . .

It looked as if she would have to endure being pampered, whether she wanted to be or not.

Five minutes later Uzziah was leading her back along the wide corridor, stopping at a heavily carved wooden door about twenty metres from his own.

'Omar will have had these quarters prepared by now,' he stated formally. 'I trust you will have a sound sleep and wake refreshed for the evening ahead. I am greatly looking forward to your company over dinner.' With that he picked up her hand and kissed it.

Beth would have loved to snatch her hand away, if she could have done so without offending him. She still stiffened inside as his flesh met hers. But then, quite unexpectedly, his kissing her hand wasn't as icky as she had thought it would be. She stared down at the way her host's lips moved with silky moistness against the back of her hand, both fascinated and appalled by the electric tingles that began racing up her arm and down her spine.

Now she did snatch her hand away. His head jerked up and, for a moment, he frowned at her, but then he smiled a wry little smile, turned and strode away.

Beth scuttled into the room and shut the door behind her, leaning back against it with a shudder. She squeezed her eyes shut, groaning her dismay as an embarrassing heat burnt into her cheeks. Oh, God, she had made a right fool of herself, over-reacting like that. Truly, she had to remember that she wasn't in Australia now, that around here, hand-kissing was probably as common as saying, 'see yuh'.

Nevertheless, did lack of hand-kissing experience entirely explain her *physical* reaction to her host's touch? Maybe she wasn't as immune to his sex appeal as she had thought?

No... That couldn't be it. She dismissed the thought at once. She was just a complete clot, with no social sophistication at all, flustered by a gesture that meant nothing to such a man. Uzziah obviously liked acting the part of a gentleman.

Well, at least he hadn't seemed too offended by her silly behaviour. He had smiled, hadn't he?

Yes, but only after he had frowned. She would have to try hard over dinner to make up for any lost ground. Uzziah wasn't likely to look favourably at a guest who kept turning her nose up at him. First there had been his murals. Now, his manners.

Beth sighed, thinking this visit was proving more complicated than she'd ever envisaged. But when she finally opened her eyes, any niggling worries were pushed aside as she glanced around the guest-room and its surprising décor.

For it held not a hint of Morocco, being totally Victorian, with a four-poster bed, heavy oak bedside chests, brass lamps and a flowered carpet on the parquet floor. There was a very cosy sitting area at the far end of the long rectangular room, complete with two small brocade sofas—facing each other across a coffee-table—a writing desk against the wall and a bookcase alongside it full of leatherbound editions.

Beth levered herself away from the door and wandered around the charming room, checking behind the two doors leading off it. One opened into a large dressing-room in which her clothes were neatly hanging; the other revealed an old-fashioned Victorian bathroom, though she suspected the plumbing was all new.

Uzziah had obviously gone to a lot of trouble with this suite, Beth guessing it was his mother's when she visited. It had English lady written all over it.

Beth frowned. It was darned hard to picture Uzziah with an English lady as a mother, yet she had little trouble seeing him in the role of an Arab sheikh's son. Still, she had to admit that if one shut one's eyes to his unusual clothes and hairstyle, his polished voice and manners could easily fit a distinguished English gentleman in a pin-striped suit with an office in Fleet Street, a manor-house in the country and a team of polo ponies in his stables.

Maybe she was being one-eyed and prejudiced by continuing to believe he was basically a barbarian, just because he dressed and looked different.

It wasn't till much later, when she was lying down on the huge bed, resting, that Beth remembered Aisha. Immediately, her whole inside tightened. If Uzziah was actually making love to the girl in his private quarters right now, then he *was* a barbarian, through and through!

Was he? came a counter argument from the voice of logic. How was such behaviour any different from that of those English noblemen who bedded the chambermaids? Or any different from Vernon's, for that matter? Dear old Vernon, who used the power of his wealth and God-given looks to seduce every woman he fancied without so much as a scrap of true caring and commitment.

OK, Beth decided magnanimously. So maybe Uzziah wasn't a barbarian. He was, however, another Vernon, which was almost as bad!

Hold on there, that irritating voice piped up again. You're not absolutely *sure* Uzziah wanted to see that girl later for sexual reasons. Maybe he only wanted to discuss a work-related matter.

A scornful and cynical laugh punched from her throat. Truly, Beth! How naïve can you get?

Not that she would ever know the truth. She could hardly lean over to him at dinner and say, 'Oh, and by the way, Uzziah old chap, did you have a nice time with Aisha earlier on? How is she in the sack, eh what? Better than me, I'll warrant.'

Beth chuckled with black humour. Just as well she wasn't a servant girl in this place. She wouldn't have a job for long if sexual skills came into it, that was for sure.

She smiled wryly at the unlikely scenario of herself in Aisha's place, meekly following Uzziah's orders to take off her clothes and join him. A dry laugh escaped her. She didn't think he'd ask her a second time. Vernon hadn't.

'You just aren't courtesan material, old girl,' she muttered out loud. 'Best stick to what you do best. Riding horses.'

A yawn captured her mouth and she snuggled into the downy quilt. Best have a little nap, too. You don't want to be falling asleep at the dinner table. Whether you like Uzziah or not, you have to present a smiling face in his presence, otherwise you might as well pack up and go home right now!

Beth woke with a start. Was that a door closing? *Her* door?

She sat up, swinging her bare feet out from under the quilt and down on to the carpet. Throwing back the bedclothes, she stood up, dragging on her pink chenille dressing-gown as she hurried over to the heavy wooden door. Opening it, she peered down the long, wide corridor.

Empty.

At the far end were the double doors that led into Uzziah's private quarters.

Beth was actually wondering if Aisha was in there right now when one of the doors opened and the girl herself came out. Aisha shut the door quietly, then turned to lean with her back against it.

What she did then staggered Beth.

The girl's hands came up to cup her breasts through her white blouse, her eyes shutting in an attitude of sensuous abandon. She stayed that way for several seconds before suddenly giving a soft whoop of delight and running off.

Beth's head shot back inside, her heart racing with a type of shock. Well! There was no doubt *now* what had just gone on in Uzziah's private quarters. None at all! And Aisha had certainly enjoyed the proceedings. Never had Beth seen such a blatant display of sexual pleasure. Why, the girl had no shame, no pride, no morals! She was nothing but a...a...

Struggling to find a suitable word, Beth slammed the door quite violently. Spinning round, she marched across the room and into the bathroom where she caught a glimpse of her flushed and angry face in the mirror.

It brought her up with a jolt. Why was she so agitated by what she had just seen? If Aisha was willing to go to bed with her employer—and who could doubt her willingness after the way she'd just acted?—then why should it bother her?

Surely she couldn't be *jealous* of the girl, could she?

Beth frowned darkly at herself.

Maybe, she decided with brutal honesty. Just maybe...

Not because of the man Aisha had just been with. Beth could not possibly be wanting Uzziah. How could she possibly want *any* man like that when she'd found sex so dismayingly boring?

Clearly, however, this was not the case with Aisha. This girl enjoyed sex, enjoyed her woman's body.

Beth had accepted all along that her failure to find pleasure with Vernon had probably been her own fault, but never had it been brought home to her so strongly as a moment ago. No longer could she pretend that other women exaggerated about the pleasure to be found in making love. No longer . . .

She pulled a face at her reflection. 'You really are frigid, Beth Carney. That's the truth and you're going to have to live with it!'

She was still looking at her unhappy face in the mirror when there was a soft tap-tap on the bedroom door.

CHAPTER FIVE

BETH glanced at her watch. It was seven o'clock. Dinner was not till eight, so it couldn't be someone coming to fetch her.

Tightening the sash on her dressing-gown, she went to open the door.

It was Aisha, holding a Polaroid camera in one hand and an armful of clothes in the other. She gave a little curtsy. 'Sidi Uzziah... he asked me to bring this to you, *mademoiselle*.' The camera was extended forward.

Beth took it. 'Thank you,' she said somewhat stiffly, all the while doing her best to quell the quite unreasonable resentment she was still feeling for this girl who was more woman than she would ever be. Managing a cool smile, she was about to retreat inside her room when Aisha spoke again.

'But *mademoiselle*... these are for you too,' she said, a worried frown on her lovely face as she held up the three hangers that had been draped over her left arm.

Beth stared at them.

The first garment was a full-length caftan made in silver-threaded emerald silk, heavily braided around the neckline, sleeves and hem. The other two hangers appeared to be carrying similar garments, one in black and another in gold, all shot with the same shimmering silver thread.

'To wear at dinner, *mademoiselle*,' the girl explained. 'It is the custom here.'

Beth felt a burst of frustration. Was she to be plagued with Uzziah's *customs* the whole weekend?

Just do as he asks, you little ninny, the voice of common sense piped up inside her head. You have nothing to lose and everything to gain!

'Very well,' she agreed with a sigh, and took the hangers, thinking she'd probably look a right idiot in such tizzy clothes. Let's hope she wasn't expected to wear all three dresses at once! Shaking her head, she was about to retreat for the second time when Aisha stopped her once more.

'But *mademoiselle* ... I ... I must come in too. I am to help you bathe and dress. Sidi Uzziah ... he will be very annoyed with me if I don't.'

The anxiety and appeal in the girl's face obliterated Beth's lingering resentment. Besides, it was hard not to like this doe-eyed sweetie with her soft French accent and engaging manner, regardless of how she spent her afternoons.

'Well, we can't have that, can we?' Beth smiled ruefully, and Aisha beamed her relief. 'But no more of this *mademoiselle* business. If I can call you Aisha then you can call me Beth. Fair enough?'

Aisha looked doubtful. 'Beth,' she said slowly. 'It is a very pretty name.'

'So is Aisha. And so are you.'

Aisha blushed and touched her dark hair. '*Non*. I am too short. Too dark. I wish to be blonde and tall ... like you.'

Now Beth laughed. Were women never satisfied with themselves? How could this delightful creature ever want to be anything other than what she was?

Why, she was everything Beth imagined a woman should be. Dainty and graceful, yet at the same time lush and sensual.

Still, it was good to find out that Aisha did not think her looks perfect. It made Beth feel better about herself.

'And *I* would like to be small and dark,' she returned with an amused smile. 'But we are what we are, Aisha, and nothing will change that. Come on in, then, and tell me which one of these glamorous-looking gowns you think would suit me best?'

'Oh, *mademoiselle*,' the girl gushed, immediately forgetting the request to call her Beth. 'There is no...how you say...question? The gold...on you it will look...*très magnifique!*' And she kissed the air in a very French gesture.

'*Très magnifique!*' Aisha exclaimed again fifty minutes later.

Beth wouldn't have gone that far, but she had to admit she looked better than she thought she would. The gold colour certainly did complement her blonde hair, and, while nothing could disguise her height, the long, ethereal gown had given to her athletic body an air of soft femininity that was usually lacking.

She held her arms out wide, admiring the way the movement set the silver threads all a-shimmer. She had never worn a caftan before, but it was the most comfortable garment, the wide sleeves and loosely flowing lines leaving one's body without constriction. Neither did it show if one was wearing underwear or not, which nullified Aisha's argument that a bra and panties would make ugly lines against the silk.

Beth's wide mouth curved into a wry smile as she recalled Aisha's earlier efforts to get her to discard her undies. But the girl's claims that it was not 'the custom' here for a woman to wear such things under a caftan had fallen on deaf ears. Beth had never gone without a bra—let alone panties—and she wasn't about to start now!

The girl had pouted her disapproval when Beth stepped her freshly bathed and powdered body into white cotton briefs then squashed her C-cup breasts into one of the sensible sports bras she always wore. But Beth totally ignored her. There was just so far she was prepared to go. Besides, Uzziah would never know the difference. It wasn't as if he was going to lift up her caftan and look, was it?

She had compromised, however, by letting the girl brush out her long hair and do her make-up. Beth had been initially startled by the amount of eye make-up Aisha applied, a dark kohl replacing the pale blue she usually wore, not to mention lashings of mascara. The girl hadn't exactly gone light on the blusher, either. Whenever Beth felt a protest bubbling up she stifled it by recalling Omar's wise words. When in Rome...

One thing, however, was beginning to bother her.

'What about shoes?' she said at last, frowning down at her bare feet. 'Or is it the custom to go barefoot?'

Aisha waved her hands in the negative. Hurrying from the bathroom, the girl scuttled across the bedroom and into the walk-in wardrobe from where she quickly emerged with a pair of heelless silver slippers large enough for Beth's not so dainty feet. It crossed her mind as she slipped them on that if they belonged to Uzziah's mother, the woman was no more a *petite* little thing than she was.

'A perfect fit!' she announced.

Aisha beamed. 'Sidi Uzziah will be very pleased with *mademoiselle*.'

Beth worried for a second that Uzziah might think she had dolled herself up for his personal benefit. She hated to think he might react to her improved appearance the way Vernon had that night at the ball. The weekend would come to a swift and disastrous conclusion if he got out of line. Beth might want a horse, but she didn't want it that badly.

She only had to look over at Aisha, however, to discount the possibility of Uzziah making a pass at her. The girl was a stunner. And sexy as anything. A man wouldn't be looking for any more after spending a few hours with *her*, that was for sure! If by some miracle he did, he could easily have the girl come to his room later in the evening.

Nevertheless, Beth did puzzle over how strangely lacking in jealousy Aisha was. Didn't she mind that another woman was about to have dinner with her lover? Or was she so confident in her own desirability and feminine power that she knew Uzziah would never look elsewhere?

Yes, Beth accepted. That was undoubtedly it. Besides, it wasn't as though she herself was any real competition. Even done up to the nines, she was hardly God's gift to men.

Her drily amused train of thought was interrupted by a loud knocking, her eyebrows lifting at the rather impatient-sounding tattoo. If this was someone come to escort her down to dinner then they were making sure she heard them.

It was only when she saw Aisha's confused expression that Beth realised something was afoot here that wasn't the norm. Not one to waffle about, she took her slippered feet across the carpet at a fast pace and wrenched open the door.

Uzziah was standing there, busily stuffing the same black shirt he'd been wearing the other day into the waistband of the same tight fawn riding breeches. His actions drew Beth's eyes to the impressive lower half of his body and, to her horror, a warm flush started flooding her cheeks.

Startled, her eyes jerked upwards to land on her host's face, which at that moment was consumed by a black scowl. 'I do apologise, my dear Beth, but I won't be able to join you for dinner after all. I have an emergency down at the stables which requires my immediate attention.'

'An emergency? Down at the stables?' Beth felt relieved to turn her attention to something other than her host's formidable physique. 'What's happened? Can I help in any way?'

The scowl on Uzziah's face dissolved into a wry smile as his flashing black gaze swept over the gold caftan. 'I don't think you're suitably attired to help with a difficult foaling, do you?'

Her flush became a fire under his amused eyes.

'No, I guess not,' she agreed in a short tone. She'd never felt more annoyed with herself in her life. Fancy blushing like some silly adolescent. And fancy feeling disappointed that he hadn't made some compliment over the way she looked.

'I must go. Aisha,' he commanded, on seeing the girl in the background, 'bring *mademoiselle* a tray to her room and get her anything else she might want. My apologies again, Beth.'

'Don't worry about me,' she said quickly. 'I'll be fine. I'm used to my own company. I like it.'

He bowed slightly, a faint smile on his face. 'Till seven in the morning, then. That's when I go riding. You still wish to accompany me, I take it?'

'I wouldn't miss it for the world,' she said quite sincerely.

The faint smile turned wry. 'Good.' With that, he whirled on the heels of his black riding boots and was away, striding down the corridor.

Beth stared after him for several seconds, troubled by that parting smile. It had been distinctly ironic, as though she had amused him in some way.

Finally, she shrugged dismissively, then turned to face Aisha, who was looking crestfallen.

'Oh, *mademoiselle*... What a shame! All that trouble for nothing.'

'Such is life, Aisha,' Beth said, feeling quite disappointed herself for some unaccountable reason. She should have been only too glad not to have to put up with Uzziah's chauvinistic company more than she had to. Why, he hadn't even had the good grace to say how nice she looked. Typical selfish male!

She threw Aisha a considering look. Poor thing. Fancy having to put up with such a man. Still ... she was probably in love with him, more was the pity.

Love ...

Now there was a four-letter word if ever there was one!

Beth shook her head in amazement at the treatment some women put up with in search of the Holy Grail called love. Perhaps Aisha thought Uzziah would fall in love with her if she slept with him. Maybe she hoped her employer would even marry her.

Experience told Beth that would never happen. She recognised the Vernons in this world only too well and this one was definitely a Vernon. He just came in a different guise.

But there was no hoping that Aisha would listen to any advice she gave. The girl came from a different world and a different culture where men ran the show and women were indoctrinated to think they were only there to serve and please.

And you think Australian society is any different? came the cynical thought. *Or Australian men?*

Beth sighed. 'Come on, then, Aisha. You might as well help me get all this paraphernalia off again.'

'*Oui, mademoiselle,*' the girl said, and hurried forwards.

'Hey! Didn't I tell you to call me Beth?'

Aisha's frowns were almost as bewitching as her smiles. Beth could well understand how her host might be besotted with the girl. But did that give him the right to use her so shamelessly? Anger rose in her breast. She would have liked to give her host a piece of her mind. Too bad she would never get the chance.

'*Oui,*' Aisha sighed. 'But if Sidi Uzziah hears me he might not like it.'

'Oh, to hell with Sidi Uzziah!' Beth pronounced, and set about getting undressed.

When the knock came on her door at a few minutes past seven, Beth was ready. In truth, she had been ready for quite some time. But as she walked towards the door she was surprised to find that her earlier feeling of excited anticipation had changed to an odd tension.

The sudden constriction in her chest surprised her. Surely she wasn't nervous about going riding with Uzziah, was she?

But any unexpected nerves were soon forgotten when she swept open the door and saw what her host was wearing *this* time.

This had to be his buccaneer look, she decided drily once she got over the initial shock. Skin-tight riding breeches made of soft black leather, topped by a full-sleeved shirt of dazzling white silk, both anchored at the hip by a wide black leather belt with a huge silver buckle. All he needed was a cutlass hanging by his side, or a patch over his eye, and he'd be able to audition for the role of Captain Blood!

Truly, the man was an incorrigible showman. Or was the word show-off? Still, she had to admit that he carried off his highly exotic taste in clothes with style, and without ever appearing self-conscious.

'Good morning,' he said, an all-encompassing glance taking in everything about *her* from her tightly knotted hair and totally un-made-up face down past her red blouse and grey, stone-washed jeans to her tan, elastic-sided riding boots.

Not a word of comment passed his lips on her appearance, though she had the impression he was slightly taken aback. What had he expected? That she would go riding in full make-up, with her hair flowing loose? Beth supposed he was used to women making themselves attractive for him—even at seven in the morning—but she wasn't one of them!

'Good morning,' she returned, her smile feeling very stiff by now.

But he didn't appear to notice, his answering smile showing teeth as dazzlingly white as his shirt. His eyes smiled as well, glittering lights dancing in their ebony depths. She found herself staring into them.

'I trust Aisha looked after you last night?'

Beth snapped her eyes away from his, aware that the tension was back in her chest.

'Yes, thank you,' she said, making a concerted effort to sound natural. Yet underneath, she felt totally flustered.

'You weren't too bored?'

'Not at all. I read one of your lovely books.'

'Ah, yes…' And he threw a glance over her shoulder down towards the bookcase. 'I had them brought in for my mother. I'm not much of a reader myself. I tend to go in for more physical activities.'

Beth was quite sure no innuendo was intended but, still, explicit images of the kind of physical activities Uzziah indulged in with Aisha jumped into her mind. An embarrassing heat gathered in her cheeks and she was only too glad to turn away and shut the door. By the time she turned back, her outward composure was in place, but her inner confusion was growing.

What, in heaven's name, is the matter with me? she puzzled. It's not like me to have sexual thoughts like that.

'All set,' she said with a covering smile.

'Follow me, then.'

He led her through a maze of corridors and winding staircases which ended at a huge nail-studded door. The heavy iron bolt yielded with some reluctance, the door creaking back to reveal a narrow cobble-stoned pathway running between two very high whitewashed walls. A clear blue sky shone overhead, the air crisply cool as Beth stepped out into it.

She gave a little shiver which might have been caused by the cold. But she suspected it was a symptom of the tension that had been gripping her ever since she'd gone to answer her bedroom door. This strained feeling certainly hadn't been helped by Uzziah's maintaining an unnerving silence during their walk through the castle.

Beth decided to do something about it.

'Did everything turn out for the best last night?' she asked casually as they moved off again.

But her tension was only increased when he took an inordinately long time to answer.

'If you're referring to the mare and foal,' he replied at long last, 'then yes . . . eventually. But it was touch and go for a long while.'

Beth tried to dampen down a swiftly rising irritation. Of course she meant the mare and foal. What did he think she meant?

'Was it a colt or a filly?'

'Colt.'

'Aah . . . I'm partial to colts.'

'Really? I like fillies myself.'

She shot him a sharp look. Was he being facetious? Surely he wasn't *flirting* with her?

'I can only use a limited number of stallions of similar bloodlines,' he explained further as they resumed walking, and Beth breathed an unconscious sigh of relief. 'Which means I have to sell my surplus colts. It kills me to part with any of my prized Arabs, but, of course, I must.'

'But surely a stud makes its living by selling what it breeds,' she remarked sensibly, before remembering that Uzziah didn't need to make money out of horses. His wealth was on tap.

'That is so, of course. But I still hate it.'

'Did you hate selling the colt I rode the other day?'

'That devil!' he scowled. 'I would willingly have given him away.'

Beth stifled a gasp of shock. *Given* away that magnificent beast? She ground to a halt and stared at him. 'But *why*? That colt was the best jumper I have ever ridden.'

Uzziah waved a dismissive hand. 'He was not pure Arabian,' he stated simply. 'I do not breed anything here but pure Arabians.'

'You don't? But I thought...I hoped...' She shrugged her confusion. 'How did you come to breed him, then?'

Uzziah's face revealed a very real annoyance. 'It is a long story and not one that pleases me, especially first thing in the morning. Come along, I would like to check the foal we were just talking about before we go riding. You have no objection to a small delay?'

'Of course not.'

'This way, then.'

Beth was left in his wake as he stalked on ahead. She quickened her stride and had almost caught him up when the confines of the high walls fell abruptly away and she found herself on the side of a hill that sloped down to a fertile valley. They were still walking down a pathway, but one which had grass underfoot and a series of white-fenced yards on either side. Each contained a sleek Arabian, either grey or bay in colour, most with foals afoot, a few still heavily pregnant.

A swift glance over her shoulder had her neck bending back to look up at the castle. From down

where she was, it looked enormous, even more formidable than from the sea.

'Is there something wrong?' Uzziah asked, having
stopped to look back at her.

'No. I was just admiring your incredible home.
Omar told me a little of its history. It's quite re-
markable, isn't it?'

'Yes. It's also remarkably private, or as private as
one can be nowadays. See those mountains in the
distance?'

'Yes?'

'They form a natural horseshoe boundary around
my *domaine*. There's no road through them, no pass.
One can only approach this place from the air or the
sea.'

Beth stared out at the mountains in awe. He owned
all the land between them and the coast? But that was
incredible! She knew he was rich, but this kind of rich
was hard to comprehend.

'Down this way,' he directed crisply, turning right
and heading towards a barn-like building at the
bottom of the hill. Actually there were a lot of barn-
like buildings dotted around the sloping green hills,
and a never-ending series of yards, all with horses in
them. Beth would have given her eye-teeth for any
one of them.

'In here,' Uzziah directed, and stood back to usher
her into the barn.

The mare and foal were in the third box along on
the left.

'Oh, isn't he a darling!' Beth exclaimed, looking
over the stall down to where the new colt was lying
in the straw, his mother nuzzling him to get up.

Uzziah went in and gave a helping hand till the foal was drinking away at its mother's teat.

'There you are, little fellow,' he crooned softly, holding the foal up with incredibly gentle hands. 'Yes, drink up... That's the way... Good boy...'

Beth found herself unbearably moved by the whole scene. Uzziah was so tender with the foal, so...caring. It was not what she had expected of him.

Vernon had always been hard on his horses. So were many of the men she knew. Uzziah, it seemed, was different. At least, where his horses were concerned. She couldn't say the same for his handling of women. In that respect, he was no different at all.

'He'll be OK,' Uzziah said when he made his way out of the stall five minutes later.

'He's beautiful.'

'Too bad he's a colt.'

'You can give him to me if you don't want him,' Beth quipped, half meaning it.

But Uzziah merely laughed. 'He's a little small for you to ride just yet. I think Flashy will be more your style.'

'*Flashy*?' she repeated as they exited the barn.

'The black colt's mother, the one you're about to ride. *That* one...'

Beth gasped when she caught sight of the jet-black mare that was being led out of another barn less than fifty yards down the path. She was very similar to her son, with the same beautiful satiny coat, and she moved the same way, dancing and prancing on the end of the reins. But she was different too. She was all racehorse, with longer, more elegant legs, and a look in her eye that spelt out a will to win, to be the best.

'That is the most beautiful horse I have ever seen,' she breathed.

'And probably the fastest,' Uzziah commented drily. 'She holds records at several race-tracks in England and France, especially for the mile.'

'That good, eh? What was her racing name?'

'Like the Wind.'

'Appropriate. Can she jump at all?' she asked, her heart in her mouth.

'Extremely well. *Unfortunately*. She's been known to kick and bite, so keep away from her extremities.'

Beth shot him a startled look. 'And you chose her for me to ride?'

His smile was a challenge. 'I wanted to see if you could control the mother as well as the son. Are you game?'

'Just you watch me,' she said with a defiant lift of her chin.

His smile widened. 'Oh, I will, dear lady. Believe me . . . I will.'

CHAPTER SIX

BETH was on a high as she reined the spirited black mare in on the crest of the hill and looked back at Uzziah, who was only now reaching the base of the incline on his stocky grey gelding. Though clearly a skilled horseman, he hadn't had the flesh under him to keep up with Flashy during her charge across the softly grassed plains that stretched from the stables towards the distant, snow-capped mountains.

Beth scooped in several deep breaths of the bracing air and thought there was no greater joy than the adrenalin-pumping experience of riding a fast horse.

'I'm not sure which one of you is crazier,' Uzziah grinned as he joined her. 'You or that mad horse!'

'Flashy's not crazy,' Beth defended. 'She's just full of beans. Aren't you, my lovely?' she murmured, bending forwards to pat her glistening neck.

The mare blew out her nostrils in a very impatient-sounding neigh, as though she already resented standing still. Not that she was. Her back legs kept skittering around, her rump continually colliding with Uzziah's horse.

'What about you?' he went on, reefing the gelding out of harm's way. 'Are you crazy?'

'Only about horses.'

One dark eyebrow lifted. 'Nothing else?'

'Not that I recall. Unless you count black jelly-beans. There was a time I almost lived on them.' Not to mention every other colour jelly-bean, she thought ruefully. But those days were definitely over!

He tipped back his head and laughed. 'You are a delight, Beth Carney from Australia. A real delight.'

Beth was astonished by this highly unexpected compliment.

'So tell me,' he went on, still smiling. 'What do you think of my *domaine*?'

She shook her head, unable to find the right words. 'It's out of this world.'

'I certainly hope so. That was the idea behind buying it in the first place. We're reasonably self-sufficient, you know. Grow most of our own food.'

'Yes, I saw a lot of fields with crops in them as I rode over.'

'We also have an extensive orchard and vineyard. We even make our own wine. Of course, there are always some things that can't be grown. But we do our best.'

Beth was surprised how pleased she felt that Uzziah didn't just sit around, playing rich man's son. 'It sounds as if you work hard around here,' she commented thoughtfully.

'We certainly do. But enough of serious chatter. I'll race you to the top of that hill over there,' he suddenly announced, wheeling his horse round and dashing off before Beth could even get the mare facing in the right direction. Flashy was quick to take the bit between her teeth, however, and she set out in pursuit, her ears flat against her head, her black tail streaming as she did what she was bred to do. Race.

But Uzziah had a good lead and it wasn't till they were actually halfway up the hill that Beth passed him, whooping in triumph as she shot by. The mad dash had almost been as exhilarating an experience as jumping the colt over that death-defying wall. But infinitely more exhausting, on horse *and* rider. Beth was quick to dismount once she had reined the mare to a halt on the crest of the hill, sliding down to the ground with jelly legs and a heaving chest.

Uzziah was only seconds behind her.

'You could have let me win,' he teased, a wry grin on his face as he brought his tired mount to an untidy halt.

She grinned back up at him, her cheeks still flushed with exertion, blue eyes sparkling.

'Sorry,' she said without any repentance at all. 'I couldn't resist.'

Uzziah stared down at her for a few moments before abruptly swinging his leg over his saddle and dismounting, landing so close to her that she rocked backwards on her heels. Her chin tipped up to look into his face and, once again, she found their eyes locked together in a strangely magnetic way.

'Neither can I any longer,' he said in a thickened voice. 'Neither can I...'

Beth was so startled by what he did next, so *shocked* really, that she let it all happen without a whimper of protest. His arms wound round her waist, drawing her hard against the heat of his body, his mouth swooping to possess hers in a kiss of quite overwhelming passion and hunger.

If he noticed the rather stunned quality of her submission, he made no concession to it. Or maybe he was used to women leaning limply against him while he worked his will upon their bodies. Beth had no idea. About *anything*. Her brain and willpower seemed suddenly useless, her body shocked into a surrender that would normally have appalled her.

Already his hands were in her hair, pulling the pins out, making it tumble down her back in wild abandon. And then he was holding her face, capturing her cheeks and chin within large, powerful hands while his mouth plundered hers with one savage kiss after another.

Gradually she grew aware of the astonishing fact that she was no longer a frozen recipient of his desire. Her heart began pounding madly in her chest, a very real heat creeping up over her flesh. She was burning up. And breathless. And totally bamboozled.

The possibility that she might be responding to Uzziah's kisses in a sexual sense was so mind-blowing that Beth immediately rejected it. What she was responding to was the flattery, she decided dazedly. She was flattered that Uzziah even *wanted* to kiss her, that he found her in any way desirable.

She had been a sucker for that once before. With Vernon.

A burst of indignation sent her wrenching backwards and glaring up into his startled face. 'What on earth do you think you're *doing*?' she raged, furious to find she was trembling uncontrollably.

'Doing?' he repeated blankly, his stunned expression showing obvious bewilderment at both her actions and her accusatory tone.

She blushed furiously, knowing full well she had let the kissing go on far too long to pretend to be a totally innocent victim. Still, she had no intention of giving ground now that she had made her stand. 'You . . . you had no right to just grab me and kiss me like that. I won't have it, do you hear?'

Both his eyebrows lifted and he folded his arms, though his eyes betrayed more wry amusement than anger. 'Come, now,' he drawled, 'don't you think this game has gone on long enough?'

She was truly taken aback. 'Game? What game?'

Now he did look annoyed, his eyes flashing with exasperation. 'Enough is enough, dear lady... So stop this play-acting immediately. It has ceased to amuse me.'

When he unfolded his arms and went to embrace her again she lashed out, her hand cracking across his face with a force only fury could summon. Uzziah stiffened, and for the first time in her life Beth felt real fear.

'I... I'm sorry,' she choked out, her chest and throat in the grip of a constriction that was as terrifying as the man glaring down at her. She dragged in a deep breath. Then another.

But it was Uzziah who exhaled loudly, one hand lifting to rub his reddened cheek. '*Are* you? Somehow I doubt that, dear lady.'

'But I am,' she groaned, her dream of buying or being given one of this man's horses disintegrating before her eyes. 'I really am.' She shook her head in a disbelieving despair. If she lived to be a hundred she would never understand the male sex. Why had he spoiled everything by kissing her just now? Why? And why did he think she'd been playing games with him? It was all very confusing and upsetting.

'So tell me,' he said, his voice curt. 'Why *did* you accept Omar's invitation to come here if you had no intention of sleeping with me? A woman doesn't agree to spend the weekend with a man of my reputation, thinking he only wants to ride horses and have dinner with her. She knows damned well what he wants!'

Beth's mouth dropped open, snapping shut only after she recovered from the shock of what he'd just said.

Yet in a way, it all made ghastly sense. Hadn't Monsieur Renault tried to warn her? But she wouldn't listen, simply because she was so sure a man like this would never want her in a sexual sense.

But he *had* wanted her. Right from the start, it seemed. That kiss just now had not been a spur-of-the-moment thing. It had been his intention all along to make love to her.

Her mouth went dry at this realisation, her eyes sweeping over his body in a scrutiny that set her heart racing anew. He was—as everyone had said—a man among men. Wealthy. Powerful. Sexy. He could have any woman he wanted. Yet he had wanted *her*, Beth Carney, the same Beth Carney who for the first twenty-five years of her life had received nothing but insults from men: insults and taunts and teasings.

A strange mixture of emotions claimed her, not the least of which was a weird joy, immediately followed by a crippling dismay.

I'm doing it again, she groaned silently. Being vulnerable to a flattery that wasn't really a flattery. Uzziah doesn't especially want *me*, Beth Carney. He merely wants something different from his usual sexual fare, someone tall and blonde instead of small and dark.

This cruel truth chilled her fluttering heart, obliterating any lingering feelings of pleasure in the fact that Uzziah had found her desirable in any way at all.

Regathering her defences, she lifted her eyes to his darkly frowning face.

'It seems we have both been labouring under a misunderstanding,' she stated coldly. 'I thought you'd asked me here as a gesture of gratitude for showing your colt to advantage. I only came because I was hoping I might have the chance to buy one of your other horses at a reduced price. When you were so nice to me, I thought... I hoped...'

She choked down the sudden thickening in her throat. 'Now I see your being nice was merely part of *your* game,' she accused derisively. 'We both made an error in judgement. I thought you were a gentleman... And you thought I *wasn't* a lady.' Her nose and chin lifted as she glared up at him. 'I should have trusted my first judgement of you.'

'Which was?'

'That you were nothing but a barbarian!'

She heard the indignant breath being sucked into his huge lungs, saw his chest expand, his shoulders square, his nostrils flare. But she was too angry now to be afraid of him.

'I wish to go back to Cairo,' she bit out. 'I trust you can arrange that?'

For an interminable time, he said nothing, merely stared at her as though he were trying to read her mind or see into her very soul. She found his penetrating gaze unnerving, but pride demanded she should not look away.

'I do not wish you to go back to Cairo yet,' he pronounced at long last.

Beth's stomach turned over. Surely he wasn't going to keep her here against her will, was he?

He kept watching her closely, his own gaze un-readable. 'I will give you the mare ... if you spend the night with me.'

Beth simply stared at him, too stunned to say a single word.

'Very well,' he sighed, 'I'll throw in an Arabian colt as well. But for that you will have to stay two nights.' His smile was sardonic. 'You won't get a better offer, especially from a barbarian.'

'You ... you must be joking!'

'Really? Omar will tell you that I am not renowned for my sense of humour.'

'But ... but what you're proposing. It's prostitution!'

'I prefer to call it ... bartering. You have something I want, and I have something you want. We come to an amicable agreement of exchange. Believe me, dear lady, if it was a call girl I wanted I could get one for a lot less than I'm offering you.'

'I don't believe this——'

'Why not? Now that you've got over your initial shock, do you really find going to bed with me such an unattractive proposition? Come, now ... you're hardly a shy young virgin. I dare say you've had quite a few lovers over the years, none of whom you've stayed with otherwise you wouldn't be tripping around the world on your own. What did any of them leave you with, except perhaps a pleasant memory? This time, you'll walk away with nearly half a million dollars' worth of horseflesh.'

Beth was both shocked and appalled. For she was tempted. She was actually *tempted*! And the laugh would really be on him, wouldn't it? Clearly he thought he'd be getting an experienced partner for the weekend, a woman of the world who would know how to cater to all his undoubtedly sophisticated desires. Instead, he would be getting *her*!

She smothered her perverse amusement with great difficulty. Little did he know that the main reason for her turning down his offer was not the morality angle—though that played a part—but the fear of embarrassment, of being made to look an inadequate fool.

'I'm afraid I must turn down your generous offer,' she said caustically.

It was hard to interpret that small, enigmatic smile he could sometimes produce.

'I rather thought you might, which leads me to my next offer. You Australians like to gamble, don't you?'

Beth was startled. What was he getting at *now*?

'I can see you're riveted, so here's my offer. I propose a race. A horse-race . . . with you and myself as the jockeys. You can have first choice of any horse I have here. I will select my mount from the remainder. The distance marked out will be one mile. If you win, you get the two horses previously mentioned and immediate transport back to Cairo. If you lose . . . you will spend the remainder of the weekend with me, as my mistress. You will dress to please me. You will be attentive and willing. You will deny me nothing.'

'But . . . but that's crazy! Why would you make such a one-sided bet? You know I can't lose if I choose to ride Flashy.'

'Jockeys have been known to fall off,' he pointed out drily.

'Not me.'

He shrugged. 'In that case you should jump at the chance. You'll be on a sure thing.'

Beth frowned. Pete had two favourite sayings. There were no such things as a sure thing, or a free lunch. She had come here, thinking the latter was true, only to find out it wasn't. Now her host was daring her to test the truth of the former saying.

But surely Pete was making a generality, she began reasoning with care. Flashy *was* a sure thing.

Beth gnawed worriedly at her bottom lip. No...there was *always* a risk connected with racing an animal.

But a champion racehorse against an Arabian? There was no real contest and she knew it. The only mystery was why Uzziah was making such a ridiculous bet. What could he possibly know that she didn't?

'I presume you won't be riding that gelding,' she said, eyes narrowing suspiciously.

'No.'

That was telling her a lot. He probably had some big brute of a stallion stashed away somewhere who could really cover the ground. But not as fast as a sixteen-hand racehorse whose speciality was the mile. There had to be some other factor she wasn't aware of which would make the contest more equal.

'Flashy has already had two gallops this morning,' she argued. 'She won't be as fresh as your new mount.'

'Rest her, by all means. We'll schedule the race for three this afternoon.'

'You're the one round here who's crazy!' she exclaimed in frustration.

'Is it a bet or isn't it?' he demanded, showing impatience at last.

Beth hesitated. Logic told her to jump at the chance, but experience warned her that a man didn't like to lose to a woman, especially one who'd just been insulted by the woman in question.

Uzziah was acting like a fool.

Yet he wasn't a fool...

She was still mulling things over when he actually voiced her concerns. 'You think I don't stand a hope in Hades of beating you. You're wondering what the catch is.'

'Wouldn't you?'

'Naturally.' He moved to stand with his feet apart, his hands on his hips in a typically arrogant male fashion. His voice, when he spoke, was almost sneering in its condescension. 'Let's just say I would pit my horsemanship against a woman's any day.'

That did it! 'Right,' she snapped. 'You're on.'

He smiled, and straight away she knew she'd made a big mistake. He'd thrown her a red herring just now by challenging her female pride and, vain idiot that she was, she had fallen for it.

'Uzziah...I...um...'

His face hardened. 'It's done, Beth. There will be no backing out. I will honour my wager if I lose. And you will honour yours. Now I think we'd best make our way back to the stables. The morning is flying by and I wouldn't want you claiming your horse wasn't rested enough. You yourself might like to rest as well. I have a feeling you might be having a very late night...'

CHAPTER SEVEN

'ALL set?' Uzziah rapped out.

Beth gulped, then glared over at him. She had been right about his producing an impressive stallion to ride in the race. His mount was a magnificent bay, slightly larger than the normal Arabian, with long strong legs and huge hindquarters.

'Not yet,' she muttered. Flashy was in a highly skittish mood. Once again, she had swung round to be facing in the wrong direction.

At least the mare hasn't been sedated, came Beth's savagely rueful thought.

She wouldn't have put it past Uzziah. The man had no conscience or moral qualms. Clearly, he would do just about anything to get his way.

'Give me a moment to get my horse straight,' she demanded, determined not to let the devil sneak a start this time. It would give her great pleasure to have Flashy streak away right from the jump, after which Uzziah could eat her dust for the rest of the race. Besides, a good start would eliminate any possibility of any rough stuff. She didn't trust him not to try to get her off balance by bumping into her, especially round the two sweeping corners on the track they'd chosen to race on.

It was a simple dirt road that followed the riverbank, just wide enough for two horses to race abreast. Uzziah had marked off an approximate mile, scraping a starting line in the dirt with a stick and putting a red flag on a tree to denote the finishing line. Beth had told him she wanted no curious on-lookers—their second ride together in one day had already brought smirking grins from the stable-hands—so this was all taking place some distance from the stables.

'Damn it,' she muttered under her breath when the black mare simply refused to face the front. Nothing worked. Not even a sharp tug of the bit combined with a good kick in her flanks.

'Having trouble?' Uzziah remarked drily, and edged closer on the bay. 'Care to use my whip?'

A sharp retort was forming on her lips when Flashy suddenly reared.

Beth's glance was vicious. 'What have you done to this horse?'

Uzziah lifted a single sardonic eyebrow. 'Not a thing. You have my word.'

'*Your* word? Huh! And what is that worth?'

'You'd better hope it's worth a small fortune in horseflesh.'

Her head snapped round. 'What do you mean by that?'

His shrug was aggravatingly nonchalant. 'If my word isn't any good then it won't matter if you win or lose, dear lady. I'll have you anyway.'

'You . . . you wouldn't!'

'Wouldn't I? I'm a barbarian, remember? Barbarians don't follow the rules of civilised society. They take what they want through force, if they can't get it any other way.'

Beth paled visibly. 'If you try anything of the kind, I'll kill you,' she vowed.

Uzziah threw back his head and laughed. 'I'm sure you'd try.'

'Uzziah,' she croaked. 'You...you can't really mean you would...would...'

His laughter dissolved into a sardonic smile. 'Don't worry. Such a situation won't eventuate. I'm going to win. And then...' He brought his horse very, very close to hers and leant over. 'Then...' he repeated, his voice dropping to a low, husky whisper '...I'm going to legitimately claim my prize.'

Beth's breath caught in her throat, a type of panic filling her mind and her heart as she looked into his cruelly handsome, smugly arrogant face. What if she *did* lose? What if the unthinkable happened? Oh, God...

But you're *not* going to lose, came the voice of common sense. You're just as good a rider as he is and you have the faster horse.

Suddenly, all hell broke loose. Uzziah's mount started rearing up and down, whether from his rider's instigation or not Beth could not be sure. But Flashy reacted badly, rearing herself, then throwing her head around wildly in an effort to bite her rider.

Beth had had enough. The waiting back in her room had been interminable, stretching her nerves to breaking point. And now...now she was having to put up with Uzziah's unscrupulous gamesmanship. Clearly, he was trying to upset her horse as well as herself.

Her blue eyes narrowed with bitter resolve. Little did he know that she was at her best when cornered, especially by a member of the opposite sex. Gritting her teeth, she took a savage hold of the wayward horse beneath her and literally forced the animal round in approximately the right direction.

'Ready!' she shouted, then added 'Go!', simultaneously spurring the mare into a gallop.

Flashy did shoot forwards, but not with her usual explosive dash. It didn't take Beth long to realise that something was definitely awry with her. She wasn't putting her heart and soul into the race, and Uzziah's bay stallion was right on her hammer.

It was maddening in the extreme. Beth urged the mare on with vigorous hands and heels riding, shouting into her ear with the same voice she used on a couple of recalcitrant riding mounts she had at home. Flashy responded in a similar fashion. By totally ignoring her and continuing at her own pace, which would have done an ordinary hack proud, but not a record-breaking racehorse.

Round the first bend they went, red dust flying in their wake. Flashy was still a good length in front, which actually worried Beth. Any Arabian worth its salt should have been able to take the lead at this speed, especially one as big and powerful as Uzziah's bay.

Perhaps he was conserving the stallion for the final dash up the straight, she reasoned. Or maybe she was going faster than she realised. Perhaps she was just getting used to the mare's speed, as one did after a while when driving a superb car. Flashy had a fluid action, her long legs covering the ground with great strides.

Beth had no time to ponder any further, for they were coming round the second and final bend, that fluttering red flag only two hundred yards away. Suddenly, the one-length lead she had was not nearly enough. She could see the stallion's head and mane out of the corner of her eye, inching closer. Bile rose in her throat at the prospect of actually losing.

'Faster, you bad horse,' she hissed into Flashy's pricked ears. '*Faster!*'

The red flag was coming closer and closer. They were still in front. They *were* going to win!

Elation sent Beth's pulse-rate into overdrive. But her triumph was short-lived. Barely fifty yards from the post she heard the sharp crack of a whip, then watched with shattering despair as Uzziah and his bay shot forwards to take a neck advantage just as they flashed past the flag.

A variety of emotions rampaged through Beth as she brought the mare to a far from exhausted standstill. But the strongest was anger. He had done something to her horse. She just knew it.

Wheeling Flashy around, she urged her over to where Uzziah was getting control over *his* horse. The mare went quite eagerly, then did something to the other horse that made the penny drop for Beth.

'Good God, this horse is in *season*! You . . . you deliberately tricked me,' she accused vehemently. 'You kept saying what a difficult horse she was to handle. But that was just a ruse, wasn't it, to distract me from the truth? You're nothing but a low-down, contemptible, sneaky, rotten——'

'Barbarian?' he finished off for her.

Infuriated by his mocking tone, she leant over and snatched the riding crop out of his hands. 'No, *bastard!*' she screamed. And started hitting him around his chest and shoulders with the small leather whip.

When he grabbed the whip and tried to wrench it out of her hand she hung on like grim death. Reason was beyond her now. She was totally out of control, her temper exploding with a force she had never known before.

With face reddening and chest heaving, she fought him for the whip as though her life depended on it. They both eventually fell out of the saddles and down on to the ground, scrabbling around in the dirt. Beth ended up flat on her back with Uzziah straddling her hips, his weight anchoring her firmly to the ground. Her arms and hands were still free, however, and there was no way she was going to yield that whip.

But he was much stronger than she was. Slowly and inexorably, he uncurled her fingers and extricated the whip from her tenacious grip.

'*Bastard*,' she repeated with a sob of defeat.

'How true!' Uzziah laughed. Throwing the whip away, he brought his hands back to hold her down by the shoulders, his huge body looming over her. Only then did she notice the angry red welts in the V of his open-necked shirt.

But she wasn't sorry. She wasn't sorry at all. Her only regret was that she hadn't landed a few on his oh, so smug face.

'Let me up,' she said in a low, shaking voice.

'*After* I've had my say.'

She clenched her teeth down hard in her jaw, a mutinous expression on her face. 'I don't seem to have any choice, do I?' she scorned, sending a savage look at the way his large male hands and hard, leather-clad loins had her pinned to the ground.

'How astute of you. Now, first things first. Your accusation that I tricked you. Let me remind you that *you* chose to ride Flashy. If you'd been the wonderful horsewoman you obviously think you are, you should have noticed she was in season this morning.'

No way was Beth going to admit that she had had little to do with mares in season before. Her riding school was full of gentle geldings. Even Vernon mostly bought colts and geldings. He had never had any interest in breeding. His method was to wait till a horse showed jumping ability and then to buy it, selling it immediately if the horse ever became injured or out of form.

'You weren't riding a *stallion* this morning,' she argued.

'True. But surely you saw all the foals around. We're coming into spring here. Most of the mares are in season. You are familiar with their moods at such a time, are you not? They can become agitated around other horses and very difficult to handle. Their minds are on one thing only. You should not have chosen to ride a mare, Beth, if you really wanted to win that race.

'Certainly not Flashy,' he added with a devilish grin, 'who has a passion for my stallion, Amir, which is legendary. Perhaps I will tell you the story some time. But back to your choice of mount for the race. Dare I suggest that underneath you might not have been all that desperate to win? Maybe you like the fantasy of having a barbarian use you as his plaything!'

Beth was mortified to feel heat gather in her cheeks.

His smile was satanic. 'You know, I think there is a lot more truth in that than you will ever admit, my sweet savage. Perhaps it's up to me to discover just how much.'

His mouth slowly started to descend.

'Don't you dare!' she spat, blue eyes blazing.

He straightened, an action which unfortunately reminded Beth of the positioning of his lower half. It was most disconcerting to have his privates pressing down into her stomach that way. Disconcerting and embarrassing. Why, it almost felt as if he was...was...

'Don't I dare what?' he drawled. 'You lost the race, remember? There's no reason why I can't begin collecting immediately. Or are you in the habit of welshing on your bets?'

She stiffened beneath his mocking scorn, her face contorting into a grimace of disgust. Surely she couldn't be expected to honour such a disgraceful bet. Surely not?

'What about *your* word, eh?' he taunted. 'Or isn't it worth anything?'

Her eyes narrowed till they were surveying him through two furious slits. God, but he was hateful! She cringed at the thought of what he might do to her in bed. But what could she do? She suspected that if she did refuse to sleep with him, he *would* take her by force. And that would give him great satisfaction, she decided bitterly. Better she be a submissive partner, a coldly bored, yawningly disinterested partner. Then—like Vernon—Uzziah would be only too glad to be done with her in the morning.

Yes, that was it! She might have lost the race—and her dreams—but Uzziah would lose too.

With a great effort of will, she relaxed her tensely held body, startling her captor with a coldly impassive look. 'Of course my word is worth something,' she said frostily. 'And of course I won't welsh on the bet. But if I recall correctly, you said I was to be your mistress for the weekend. In my world, a mistress is treated with every consideration regarding her creature comforts. She wouldn't be expected to make love on some dirt road.'

His initial astonishment at her speech slowly melted into an amused smile. 'I take it I won't have to have you bound and gagged, then, to get your co-operation? You will dress to please me at dinner this evening, then accompany me afterwards to bed, without argument, without fuss?'

'You have my word.'

His black eyes took on a wariness. 'I find your meekness quite at odds with your normally high-spirited personality.'

'Don't mistake my co-operation for meekness, Uzziah,' she warned curtly. 'I bitterly resent having to put my body at the disposal of a man who treats women with such little respect. Fancy presuming that my accepting an invitation to your home invariably meant I was willing to sleep with you! Your arrogance in that regard is appalling. But this aside, I recognise that I am in my present unenviable position because of my own greed. I coveted your beautiful horses, and I was prepared to risk my pride and self-respect to own one. Now I must pay for my greed and I will do so, I hope, with my head held high and my spirit undaunted. But God help you, Uzziah, if any real physical harm befalls me tonight!'

Her uplifted chin was full of dignity. 'Now I suggest you let me up so that we can begin walking home. The horses have run off and the sun is already setting.'

Uzziah frowned down at her for several excruciating seconds before doing as she requested. Once on his feet he stretched out his hand to help her get up. She gave his offer a contemptuous glance before scrambling up under her own steam, then brushing the dirt off her clothes with slapping movements.

'One more thing,' she snapped, forgetting that she had meant to be oh, so controlled in all of this. 'I wouldn't like you to worry when I'm not transported to the heavens during our—er—time together.' Every word, every nuance was full of cynical sarcasm. 'I do realise you think you are God's gift to women, but actually, dear Uzziah, I find the thought of sex with you incredibly boring. In fact, I find the thought of sex in any shape and form incredibly boring. Do I make myself clear?'

His only visible reaction was to continue staring at her with a dark thoughtfulness. When he was still staring several seconds later, Beth began to feel unnerved. What was he thinking behind that pensive black gaze? Was he shocked? Angry? He didn't look angry. He looked almost... intrigued?

Annoyed that he hadn't reacted as she'd hoped, Beth pivoted on angry heels and began marching in the direction of the stables.

'In *my* world,' Uzziah called after her with a cavalier coolness, 'a mistress does not stomp off in a temper like a spoiled child. She waits for her lover and walks by his side, holding his hand while being pleasant and agreeable.'

Beth ground to a halt, taking a deep breath and composing her face before turning round.

'Don't push your luck, Uzziah,' she bit out.

He walked slowly towards her, an implacable look on his strongly handsome face. 'And do not push yours. It's time someone took you in hand, *madame*, and I'm just the man to do it!' He took her hand in a not too gentle hold. 'Now we may proceed, though I suggest you look a little happier, my dear. You wouldn't want Omar and the others to think we've had a lovers' tiff, would you?'

CHAPTER EIGHT

AISHA presented herself to help Beth bathe and dress, as she had the night before, uncaring, it seemed, that she was once again helping prepare some other woman for a night of intimacy with her own lover. She chattered away during the task of making Beth over from her ordinary self into a female of highly presentable—even desirable—appearance, rattling Beth with her blasé attitude.

Maybe it was readily accepted here that a man could be involved with more than one woman simultaneously, Beth excused, but *she* found the idea utterly disgusting. If she could have devised a way to get out of spending the night with Uzziah she would have willingly embraced it. But alas...nothing had come to mind, despite having sought inspiration ever since Uzziah had delivered her back to her quarters and ruthlessly locked the door.

Fighting him physically would be futile. Running away was now impossible. Suicide seemed overly melodramatic.

She shivered when she recalled how he had kissed her tightly closed lips in farewell, smiling as she drew away. 'I will excuse your lack of co-operation this once,' he'd murmured before his eyes had flashed a warning. 'But only this once...'

Beth surveyed her reflection in the cheval mirror with a bitter ruefulness. The gold caftan certainly did suit her, as did the extravagant make-up and the way

Aisha had done her hair, her long fair locks all curled then swept up in a high pony-tail which was secured with a glittering gold band. She might look as if she was fit for a harem on the outside, but underneath . . .

Beth had to stifle a fit of very inappropriate giggles. Yet it was hard not to be drily amused by the mental picture of Uzziah's face when he eventually encountered her sensible cotton underwear.

'You will dress to please me!' he'd pontificated.

Well, he could go fly a kite, she thought savagely. If he imagined for one moment that she was going to swan around without her pants on then he had another think coming! The bra was going to stay too. Who knew? They might prove to be her salvation. One look at her chaste undergarments might turn that voracious sexual appetite of his right off.

'Is there something wrong, Beth?' Aisha asked. 'You look very beautiful tonight. Sidi Uzziah will be very, very pleased.'

'Will he just,' Beth muttered, puzzling for the umpteenth time over the girl's amazing lack of jealousy.

'Do not be nervous,' Aisha said with a gentle touch on Beth's wrist. 'Sidi Uzziah . . . he is said to be a very good lover. Very . . . tender. You will not be disappointed.'

Beth stared at the girl. 'What . . . what do you mean, Uzziah is *said* to be a good lover? Don't you *know*? I mean . . . I thought you and he were . . . were . . .'

Aisha was a very intuitive girl, and quickly jumped to the right conclusion. 'You thought we were lovers? Sidi Uzziah and myself?' The girl laughed softly. '*Non.* Never. I am in love with Omar. He is my man, soon to be my husband. Sidi Uzziah decreed it so yes-

terday. He noticed, you see, that I am with child. My
bosom has—er...' She gestured that it had grown
larger. 'Sidi Uzziah guessed the truth and has ordered
Omar to marry me as soon as possible.'

'Oh,' was all Beth could think of to say. So that
was why Uzziah had stared so hard at Aisha yesterday, why he'd wanted to see her later. It also explained why Aisha had come out of Uzziah's quarters
looking so triumphant. And the touching of her
breasts... That had been more a maternal action than
a sexual one.

'I... I'm sorry, Aisha. I thought...' Beth coloured
fiercely, embarrassed and flustered by how wrong she
had got everything. She was also astonished—and
somewhat bewildered—at how pleased she felt that
Aisha was not Uzziah's mistress. Which was crazy!
How did that change the disgraceful way he had
treated her this afternoon?

But still...it *was* good of him to care about Aisha's
welfare. He could just as easily have ignored the whole
situation.

'I think *mademoiselle* likes Sidi Uzziah very much,'
Aisha said with a softly knowing smile. 'You will make
him a very happy man tonight. It has been too long
since he has had a woman in his bed.'

Beth stared at Aisha, startled by the way her heart
had leapt at this last piece of news. Could the girl be
right? Could it be that underneath all her huffing and
puffing she *was* secretly attracted to Uzziah? Or was
she still suffering from her old problem of being vulnerable to the flattery of a man's desire?

Logic brutally reminded her that if Uzziah hadn't
been with a woman for a long time then his having
chosen *her* was probably the result of frustration, not

any real desire for her as an individual or special woman.

'And how long has it been since a lady has graced his lordship's bed?' she demanded to know, her curt tone evidence of...*what*?

Surely not *jealousy*? That would imply that she wanted to be in Uzziah's bed for her own pleasure, and that just couldn't be so, she reasoned ruthlessly. Finding a man attractive and finding pleasure in his bed did not follow for her.

And yet...when Uzziah had kissed her today, hadn't she gone like mush in his arms? Then later, when he'd accused her of really wanting to lose the race, hadn't a wild alien heat surged through her veins?

'Oh, a long time,' Aisha was saying. 'Nearly a month, I think.'

Beth snapped out of her bewildering thoughts to stare at the girl. 'A *month*!' she gasped.

'Yes, yes, a very long time,' the girl said quite seriously.

Beth could hardly believe her ears. Aisha thought a mere *month* was an inordinately long time for a man to go without sex? Good grief! Still, she supposed this was the land of harems and Muslims, where a man could have up to four wives, and where his pleasure was a woman's first concern. But *still*!

She frowned at a sudden thought. 'Is Uzziah a Muslim?'

Aisha looked oddly aghast, shaking her head vigorously in the negative.

'A Christian, then?' Beth tried.

Aisha was, if anything, more appalled. 'Sidi Uzziah—he has no religion. Please...do not bring up this subject in his presence. Religion is one of the two subjects that can make him go...poof!' Aisha threw up her hands in an explosive gesture.

Beth's blue eyes widened. 'And what is the other subject that makes him go poof?'

'Marriage.'

'But what has he got against marriage? He wants Omar and you to marry, doesn't he?'

The girl shrugged. 'He is not easy to understand...'

'You can say that again.'

'But he is a good man. A kind man.'

Good? Kind? Who did Aisha think she was kidding? The man was a profligate, a libertine, a rake and a scoundrel!

He was also the man Beth was about to spend the night with, only the second man in her life with whom she had done so.

What if he did laugh at her? she worried anew. What if he found her frigidity a big joke? She could bear just about anything, but not scorn.

'Aisha,' she said abruptly, then hesitated. 'I...I think I might take off my underwear after all...'

The girl beamed her approval.

Beth had just completed the hurried task and drawn the caftan back over her head when there was a restrained knock on the door.

'That will be Omar come to escort you to dinner,' Aisha informed her. 'Here. Let me fix those few strands of hair that have escaped. There...now you are ready...'

Ready?

Beth gulped, then took one last glance in the mirror. Was this how Gigi had felt that night when she was to make her début as Gaston's mistress? If she had,

then Beth could well understand her nervous prayers.
She herself felt sick with nerves.

Gigi had prayed that if the coming night was to be
her Waterloo, then she wanted to be Wellington. That
was all very well for Gigi, Beth thought ruefully. Such
a warm, beautiful woman had some *hope* of being
Wellington. Beth knew exactly which one she would
turn out to be tonight. Napoleon!

Such thinking revived memories of how she had felt
the morning after her night with Vernon. She'd woken
to find him standing in the doorway of his en suite,
towelling his hair dry, not even bothering to hide his
nakedness. Or his disappointment in her.

'You're not exactly a bundle of passion, are you,
sweetheart?' he'd drawled. 'Maybe you left it too long
to get started. Look, you'd better toddle off home
now. It's getting late and I'm expecting another—er—
visitor shortly.'

He'd turned away then, and gone back into the
bathroom. Beth had crawled out of the bed and into
her clothes, then crawled on home. She vowed later
that day never to crawl anywhere because of a man
ever again.

That vow came back to her now, as well as a good
degree of self-righteous anger. Uzziah had had no right
to trick her into such a disgracefully unfair bet this
afternoon, nor to demand she honour it afterwards.
But then, he had no honour. None at all!

Hardening her heart, she walked to where Omar
was waiting patiently for her, all her earlier softening
towards Uzziah well and truly gone.

Omar's expression, when he saw her, could have
been flattering if she'd been in the mood for flattery.
She wasn't.

'Miss Carney!' he gushed. 'How lovely you look. Sidi Uzziah . . . he will——'

'Yes, yes. He will be very pleased. So Aisha has already informed me.'

Her curtness brought a frown from Omar.

'Is everything all right, Miss Carney?'

'Of course,' she returned coldly. 'What could possibly be wrong?'

Omar's expression was definitely one of dark puzzlement.

The lengthy walk down the corridor only served to remind Beth of her nakedness underneath the caftan. The thin material clung to her thighs, her unfettered breasts undulating beneath the gold silk. By the time they reached the carved doors that guarded Uzziah's private quarters, her heart was pounding angrily within her chest, friction having hardened her nipples till they were jutting out like bayonet tips.

And to think she had once imagined a caftan was an exceptionally modest style of dress!

Infuriated at the whole embarrassing situation, Beth glared at the closed doors, a bitter cynicism invading her heart as Omar knocked. Of course there had never been any doubt where this evening's dinner would be held. This was not an occasion for the grand dining-hall, or the ballroom, both of which Uzziah had pointed out to her during their tense return walk through the castle earlier in the afternoon. This meal was always going to be consumed within easy reach of the *master's* bed.

Omar waited only a few seconds, then threw the doors open, startling Beth when she saw immediately that there were flaws in her presumptions about the evening ahead. For they were not to be alone, as it turned out. A small group of musicians were limbering up their instruments in a far corner of Uzziah's sumptuous living-room, their instruments—as well as their sounds—quite foreign to her. There appeared to be a set of odd-looking drums, a type of tambourine, a fatly rounded guitar, and a wind instrument that might have been a flute, but looked too small.

'Come and sit down, Miss Carney,' Omar directed. 'I must go and see if my master needs me.'

He led her over to the low-slung purple divan that stretched behind the largest of the equally low tables. Sinking down into the plush velvet cushions, Beth tried not to gape at the dinner setting before her. But, my goodness, she had never seen such beautiful crockery and cutlery. The plates were the finest white china, edged in what she suspected was real gold.

The cutlery was gold too. Real or not, it was still magnificent, with an elegant, scrolled design on the handles. As for the wine goblets and decanters... They were simply breathtaking, made in the most delicately blown glass, their mauve colour deeper at the base, diffusing to a clear glass by the time it reached the rims.

Beth was impressed, despite her underlying irritation. Till she reminded herself that such trappings meant nothing to an oil-rich sheikh's son. He'd probably been eating off gold plates all his life!

Her chin lifted with a scornful sniff, her eyes darting around the opulent room, looking for more evidence to fuel her antagonism towards Uzziah. If she stopped to think, Beth might have worried over why she kept needing reason upon reason to keep disliking the man so vehemently.

'Oh,' she gasped when a dark figure suddenly loomed into an archway on her right.

It took her only a fleeting moment to realise it was Uzziah. With recognition of who it was standing there, staring over at her, Beth's heart not only jolted back into life, it started to race.

She didn't want to stare back at him. But she did.

He too was wearing a caftan-style robe, but, where hers was glitzy and gold, his was satanic black and starkly plain, with a hood that was drawn up over his head, hiding his hair and casting shadows across his face. He looked enigmatic and mysterious and extremely dangerous.

For what seemed like ages he simply stood there, his deeply set ebony eyes surveying her own appearance with a heavy-lidded gaze. When he still hadn't moved almost a minute later, her irritation resurfaced with a vengeance. Was this some well-tried seduction technique? she wondered caustically. Was this long, searing look supposed to set her heart pounding and her thighs trembling with anticpation?

Your heart *is* pounding, some inner voice drily reminded her.

From fury, she snapped back to herself in silent rebuke.

Lifting a sardonic eyebrow, she decided to give him a dose of his own medicine, her own gaze moving slowly down his half-hidden face, lingering on the cruel cut of his mouth before continuing to nonchalantly inspect the rest of his body. Though to be honest, not much of it was on display.

The neck of the robe was high and round with a narrow slit down the centre, showing only a hint of his hairless, olive-skinned chest, and nothing at all of his impressive muscle structure. Though admittedly, not even clothes could hide the breadth of that chest, nor the broadness of his shoulders. Still, the rest of him was hidden from her eyes, the long sleeves wide and full, the lower half of the robe falling in covering folds down to his slippered feet.

Suddenly his hands moved to push the sleeves up his arms a fraction, then to flick back the hood. He simultaneously walked forwards, striding across the marble floor, signalling to the musicians to start as he came.

Now Beth was really staring—at his hair, which was no longer confined. While still slicked back from his forehead, the rest flowed loosely down to his shoulders in glossy black waves. These lifted and rippled as he walked, glinting under the lights of the chandelier above.

But it wasn't just Uzziah's free-flowing hair that drew her startled attention. The act of walking—as it had with her own caftan—was drawing the black linen more tightly across his thighs, outlining their strength and power. Her stomach churned at the realisation she wasn't the only one in this room without underwear.

Beth just managed to regather her wits—and close her gaping mouth—before he actually joined her. But confusion still reigned within her thudding heart till she finally accepted that Uzziah was one of those extremely virile, sexually charged men who could evoke a primitive physical response from any woman, even one who'd learnt to suppress her desires because she couldn't bring them to a natural fruition.

This thought soothed her bewildered brain somewhat, and she was able to look at the man sinking down into the divan beside her without panicking at her fluttering insides.

In this at least, I am normal, she hugged to herself with some satisfaction. I can still be sexually attracted to a man. I just can't seem to transfer that attraction from my mind to my body. Somewhere along the line, there's a break in my circuits.

'You're looking ravishing tonight, my dear Beth,' he said in that suave English accent of his. Before she could stop him, he swept up her hand and pressed it to his lips. She did not try to hide her somewhat ambivalent shudder, though he merely ignored it, keeping her flesh against his mouth a few moments longer, glancing up at her from under arched eyebrows as he parted his lips slightly, sending his tongue tip forwards to graze over her skin.

Her teeth clenched down hard in her jaw in a futile attempt to stop the tempestuous feelings that were threatening to erupt within her.

When he finally released her fingers, she was shocked to find she was actually trembling. It sent her thoughts into a veritable tail-spin. Suddenly, this man was making her think and feel and hope for things no man had made her think and feel and hope for in many long years.

It tore Beth's conscience in two. One part of her wanted to surrender to these alien feelings, to find out where they might lead. But the other half, that half where her pride and self-respect resided, demanded she keep a cool control over herself, to not give this bastard the satisfaction of knowing he could stir her senses against her will.

But is it against your will? a dark voice whispered seductively. Since Uzziah is going to make love to you anyway, why not lie back and try to enjoy it? Why not?

Because I don't love him, she argued fiercely to herself. I don't even like him!

And with that, she snatched her hand away.

Uzziah's smile was infuriatingly bland. 'Time to eat, I think.' And he clapped his hands.

Beth would have liked to refuse dinner, haughtily saying she wasn't hungry, that the thought of what she had to endure later tonight had dispelled her appetite for everything, even food. But the moment the first dish arrived—a steaming, aromatic soup which Uzziah informed her was *harira*, a traditional Moroccan soup—her taste-buds let her down. Besides, she hadn't eaten a thing all day and was literally starving.

The delicious soup was followed up by a mouth-watering plate of *matisha mesla*, an ancient Moroccan recipe in which chicken was slowly simmered in a sauce of tomatoes, honey, ginger and cinnamon. Or so Uzziah explained when it was placed before them.

'How nice,' she said with chilly politeness.

Uzziah merely smiled again, making Beth itch to throw her glass of red wine into his face. Instead, she picked it up and drank deeply.

There was more than one way to exact vengeance. If she got well and truly drunk, she would practically be unconscious by the time they went to bed. Beth suspected her smug host might not fancy that at all!

'Easy,' Uzziah warned. 'That wine is a local brew, with a high alcoholic content.'

'Is it?' Flashing him a false smile, she set her glass down on the table and refilled it from the decanter. 'Splendid.' But when she went to sweep the wine back to her lips, a large hand clamped over her wrist, stopping her midstream.

'I'm afraid I can't let you do that,' he said in a low but very firm voice. 'Intoxication dulls the senses. I want you wide awake when I finally make love to you, my dear lady. Wide awake and extremely aware.' And, taking the glass from her, he beckoned one of the servants over from where they were standing at attention against a far wall, waiting to be of service. 'Take this away and bring *mademoiselle* some mineral water,' he ordered.

'How dare you?' she spat once the servant was out of ear-shot. 'I have every right to have a drink if I want to.'

'You have no rights tonight,' he returned coolly. 'Or for the rest of the weekend. You lost them this afternoon. You are mine for the duration, to do with as I will. And I do not want you drunk.'

His very casualness infuriated her. 'And what if I choose not to honour that disgusting bet? What if I get up from this table right here and now and walk out?'

'Try it. You won't get very far.'

'And what would you do? Come on, give it to me straight. What does a barbarian do when a woman rejects him, when she tells him to his face that he revolts her, that she would almost throw up if he touched her?'

'I have no idea what a barbarian would do,' he informed her with an amused glittering in his eyes. 'I can tell you what *I* would do in the case of a certain woman who's sitting before me now, looking so desirable and sexy that I can hardly keep my hands off her, and who is, by the way, fooling herself on a large scale if she imagines for one moment she doesn't want me to make love to her.'

Beth sucked in a startled breath, her blue eyes widening.

'I would catch her quite easily of course,' he continued, his eyes locked to hers now, darkly penetrating and wickedly intent. 'Then I would carry her into my bedchamber where I would bind her to my bed with some very soft scarves so as not to bruise her lovely golden flesh. Then I would cut all the clothes from her beautiful body and oh, so gently touch her till she was quivering with desire beneath my hands. Then and only then would I let my own body speak of its longing to be as one with hers. I would not be quick, or cruel. I would love her with great tenderness, kissing her all the while, telling her of the passion and hunger that has possessed me since I first saw her. I would not allow myself release till she had sighed with pleasure beneath me over and over again...'

Beth could only stare at him, dazedly aware that her entire mouth and throat had gone dry, that her chest had contracted till it was a painful vice around her pounding heart, that her mind was being bombarded with the stunningly erotic promises he was making.

Quite abruptly he reefed his eyes away, breaking the spell he'd successfully cast over her. When they returned to her face, their expression was decidedly sardonic.

'I presume you wouldn't want any of that to happen to you, would you?' he taunted softly.

All she could do was swallow.

'I thought as much. So we can safely move on to the next course, minus the wine? You won't try to run away? Aah ... I thought not ... What a pity ... I was actually beginning to enjoy that scenario myself ...'

And he clapped his hands again.

CHAPTER NINE

Now Beth's appetite really had deserted her. She picked away at one of the selection of French pastries put before her, trying to ignore the man at her side.

Impossible. Even if she closed her eyes, she would still be intensely aware of his physical presence by the tantalising aroma of sandalwood that kept wafting from his skin. It evoked images of Uzziah lying naked on his bed while servant girls massaged perfumed oil into his freshly bathed flesh.

Beth tried in vain to stop other images from jumping into her head, but she could not, especially the highly erotic scenario Uzziah had just described in such explicit detail. Thinking about it made her go hot all over, so much so that her body felt as if it was burning up.

Was it possible to be seduced by words alone? she wondered.

No, came her intuitive answer. Uzziah hadn't used only the power of his words tonight to set her mind and body on a sexual journey. Everything he had organised so far had been with her ultimate surrender in view. The way she was dressed, the way *he* was dressed, the exquisite food, the music. All designed to stretch her nerve-endings to a heightened sensitivity so that they would clamour to be soothed. Clearly she had challenged his male ego with her declaration this afternoon that she found sex boring, and he was intent on proving her wrong.

Beth groaned silently. What a clever, devious fellow he was! And what a weak fool *she* was. Where was her self-righteous anger now? she agonised. Her feminine pride? Her resolve not to co-operate with Uzziah in the ruthless claiming of his so-called prize?

Gone, she accepted with a jab of dismay. Gone...

But could she be condemned for that? she pleaded with her conscience. Maybe this was her one chance to prove to herself that she could act and feel like a real woman. Somehow, this man—this devil!—was achieving the unachievable. He was making her want him, not with her mind, but with her body. Her flesh was clamouring for him to touch it, kiss it, arouse it further. Maybe she wouldn't find the ultimate ecstasy with him—that seemed too much to hope for—but she would not be bored.

No, came the bitterly wrung concession. Uzziah would never be boring in bed.

A shudder reverberated through her, making her fork clatter against the plate.

This brought a sidewards glance from Uzziah. 'You've hardly touched your dessert. Would you like something else instead?'

She pushed the plate away. 'No, thanks. I've had enough. I can't eat any more.' She turned and faced her protagonist with a tightly held face, her eyes drawn inexorably to his mouth. So cruel, she thought. And yet, she wanted that mouth on hers right at this very moment. The admission infuriated what was left of her already damaged pride. Why should he win her willingness as well as everything else? It was mortifying in the extreme.

No, she decided with a rush of renewed resolve. Nothing was worth having to witness this brute's smug triumph. Nothing.

I will shut my mind to these feelings. I will not respond. I will not!

'Must you drag this all out?' she snapped. 'I'd much rather we got on with it.'

His laugh was low and amused. 'Such tact! I wouldn't advise you to ever take on being a mistress as a career, Beth, my sweet. You don't seem to have the talent for it.'

'Too true. But that's your bad luck. If you end up disappointed then don't say I didn't warn you.'

'Disappointed? In you? Never. I've already had the most entertaining time this weekend that I've had in years. I knew the moment I saw you riding that black rogue of mine back in Egypt that you were a woman a man would enjoy to the nth degree. Now all I have to do is convince *you* of that fact.'

Before Beth could find a single thing to say, Uzziah clapped his hands again.

Immediately, the soft background music changed to a throbbing, pulsating rhythm, and a dancing girl burst through the open doors. Running forwards across the floor, she slid on to her knees at the base of the steps in front of them, her spine arching back so that her long black hair was spread out against the white marble. She was not an overly young woman, but still very beautiful, her voluptuous body provocatively clad in a diaphanous skirt of veils, attached to a silver sequinned band slung low around her hips, a minute matching bra barely covering her lush breasts.

Beth found it impossible to take her eyes off the way the woman started undulating her stomach, bringing attention to the jewel sparkling in her navel. Her movements were incredibly sensual, her hips gyrating in a series of slow circles, followed by some grinding pelvic thrusts.

When she finally got to her feet and began to bellydance around the room, Beth sighed with relief, a flustered heat having gathered in her cheeks at such an explicit performance. Unaware that Uzziah had been watching not the performer, but herself, Beth did not think to hide her discomfort. When she moved her head slightly and found his gaze upon her, her embarrassment was acute.

'The dancer is very good, is she not?' he said lazily. 'Very... stimulating.'

Her blush deepened, self-disgust spiking her tongue. 'I hope so. You're going to need all the help you can get.'

Uzziah laughed. 'Somehow I don't think I'm going to have too much trouble.'

'You're a bastard, do you know that?' she flared.

He shrugged nonchalantly. 'Of course. My parents, unfortunately, never married.'

'Oh, you... you know that's not what I meant!'

His laughter was irritating in the extreme. 'Naturally. Now stop complimenting me and watch the entertainment. Lalla is one of the most sought-after belly-dancers in Morocco.'

'I've no doubt,' Beth retorted acidly. 'Men are the same all over the world. All they want is the obvious.'

Uzziah leant over till his mouth was almost against her ear. 'If that was so, my little spitfire,' he whispered, 'then what do I want with you?'

Beth twisted round to stare into his eyes, fiercely aware that his mouth was only a gasp away from hers. 'I...I don't know,' she stammered. 'What do you?'

Their gazes locked, hers wide with confusion, his momentarily betraying a confusion of his own. 'You talk too much,' he growled at last, jerking angry black eyes away. 'Watch the dancer and learn what it is to be a woman.'

Uzziah muttered something further under his breath as he settled back to watch the belly-dancer, a scowl on his face.

The music gradually increased in tempo, the belly-dancer's movements becoming more and more frenzied. First, her shoulders and breasts would shake, while her head and hips remained motionless. Then her lower half would take over. Each time this happened, she tore one of the gauzy veils off and tossed it aside. Soon, she was down to little more than a very abbreviated bikini.

The climax of the dance was obviously approaching, for the music changed once more and the dancer slowly moved towards them. Her flashing dark eyes went automatically to Uzziah, her exotic face taking on a sultry expression as she undulated before him. With eyes narrowed and teeth almost bared, she dropped her head back, arching so that her long dark hair spilled away from her neck. Her stomach and pelvis began to gyrate, faster and faster, in and out, round and round. Her bejewelled navel, Beth imagined, had a life of its own, totally separate from the pale, glistening flesh that surrounded it.

The drums grew louder, pounding their rhythm right through Beth's already whirling head. Her breathing had become very shallow and rapid. She wished the dancing would stop, wished it were all over, wished Uzziah would put her out of her misery and just take her to bed. It no longer mattered what he had first seen in her or why she was here. She was. And he meant to have her. There was certainly no doubt about that!

Suddenly, there was a clash of cymbals and the dancer sprawled face down on to the floor in a dramatic finale. Uzziah began a slow clap of appreciation, but Beth just sat there stiffly, beads of perspiration on her forehead.

The woman's head eventually lifted. Darting Uzziah a sly smile, she rose in a single fluid movement, bowed, then exited, scooping up her discarded veils as she left. Almost immediately, the musicians also departed. The servants as well. The doors were discreetly closed.

All of a sudden, Beth had her wish. She was alone with Uzziah.

The silence was electric. Till he broke it.

'We will retire, I think, to the main bedchamber,' he announced quite formally, and held out his hand.

Beth stared at his hand, her stomach churning, her heart thudding. This was it. This was finally it.

Was it fear of another humiliating failure as a woman that made her do what she did? Or just fear?

Beth had no idea. All she knew was she could not willingly and meekly go through with this.

'No!' she cried out, and jumped to her feet, eyes wildly defiant. '*No!*' she screamed, and began to race for the doors.

She almost made it through them, though what good that would have done her, Beth did not know. Logic should have told her that there was nowhere really to run to, unless she was planning to throw herself from the battlements into the sea below.

'So *this* is what you wanted all along!' Uzziah grated out after he'd kicked the door shut out of her hands and pinned her hard against the solid wooden panel. 'I almost guessed your game earlier on, my sweet. Though I didn't appreciate the extent of its darkness. I actually believed you when you said you found sex boring.'

His laughter was hard and cynical. 'My male ego spurred me to think I could be the first man to show you the delights of the flesh, to teach you the beauty and wonder of making love properly. But no! That's not what you want at all, is it? You like to pretend you are not willing, because you want the man to act like a savage. It turns you on, doesn't it, to play hard to get, to goad a man so that he can think of nothing but having you? Then when you reject him and run, like you did just now, you hope he'll lose all control over his desire and take you by force.'

'No,' she croaked out, appalled at his accusations. 'That's not true!'

'Isn't it?' he sneered, bringing his face so close that she could hardly focus on his blazing black eyes. 'How come I don't believe you? God, but I've heard of women like you. I've just never met one, which is strange, since I've met every other kind of wicked, manipulative bitch this rotten world can produce. Normally I can spot them a mile off. But you . . . you got under my guard, and my skin, dammit. Much as I might want to send you right back where you came from, I can't . . .

'I just can't,' he groaned, and, pressing his body against hers, he kissed her, hotly, hungrily, scattering what was left of her wits to the winds. His mouth was like a furnace, full of a molten liquid that poured heat into her own mouth, turning it into a malleable object for the invasion of his fiery tongue. She moaned beneath its onslaught, moaned and melted, her knees going from under her, their mouths suddenly wrenched apart as she sank downwards.

He dragged her back up and held her against the door, glaring down at her swollen lips, her fiery cheeks, her desire-glazed eyes. His laugh was hard and dry.

'How is that I can despise you, yet want you at the same time? I must be mad! You like it rough? So be it!' And, with that, he swept her up into his arms and carried her swiftly across the marble floor, through the archway and into the main bedchamber.

CHAPTER TEN

HE LITERALLY threw her on to his bed. She bounced, landing in a pile of multicoloured satin cushions. She had no time to look around at the huge semicircular bed with its massive carved bedhead, or the silk drapes that hung in exotic folds from the canopy above it. Neither was she capable, at that moment, of admiring the delicate gold and crystal lights that studded the walls, or the walls themselves, covered in the most intricate tile mosaics. Her wide-eyed gaze was riveted to a furious Uzziah who even at that moment was reefing his black robe over his head, tossing it aside to reveal his naked and stunningly aroused male body.

'Oh, dear God,' she groaned, the reality of imminent rape pinning her to the bed in a frozen limbo of shock and horror.

'Prayers?' he scorned, and loomed over her, his dark waves falling around his face like a black curtain, so that the wild glittering in his eyes was the only thing she could see.

'They won't help you now,' he muttered. And, taking two bunches of gold silk in his huge hands, he ripped her caftan asunder from neckline to hem, the tattered garment swiftly joining his own discarded robe on the black marble floor.

Now Beth reacted instinctively, outrage at such violence snapping her out of her robotic state. She grabbed a cushion and began hitting him with it. 'You get away from me, you bastard!' she screamed. 'Get away! I... I'd rather die than let you touch me!'

'I'll write your epitaph,' he ground back, snatching the cushion from her hands and flinging it away so hard that it hit one of the wall lights, rattling the crystal teardrops.

She retaliated by using her hands and nails, raking the latter down over his neck, feeling no remorse when droplets of blood oozed from the long red scratches she had made. Uzziah touched his hand to his neck, then stared at the blood on his fingers, an angry red flush staining his cheeks.

'You little hellcat!' he spat. 'I'll make sure you don't do that again!' And, seizing both her wrists in a single iron grip, he hauled her arms up over her head. Beth had thought she was physically strong, but compared to this man she was as weak as a kitten, her struggles to escape his grasp quite useless.

With a snarl of raw triumph, he pressed her down into the cushions while he yanked one of the silk drapes down from overhead. Breathing heavily, he wound the long strips of cream silk round and round her wrists, then secured them to the headboard. Beth was beside herself. When her attacker went to climb back off the bed, she kicked out with her long legs, one of them landing a glancing blow to his groin. A low growl of pain punched from his lungs, his black eyes blazing as they lanced hers.

'You don't know when to give up, do you?' With a contemptuous grimace he moved his naked bulk on to the bed, straddling her hips and thighs as he had earlier that day, his body weight and position making any kicking futile. 'Now kick all you like, Miss Spitfire. I might even enjoy the sensation.'

She glared up at him, her bared breasts rising and falling in a bewildering mixture of hate and unbidden excitement.

Uzziah merely laughed.

'What an actress you are!' he exclaimed. 'Anyone would think you weren't loving it!'

And he laughed some more.

'But you are, aren't you?' he went on, his voice dropping to a roughened whisper as he leant forward to cup her full, creamy breasts, his thumbs rubbing over the tender peaks till they sprang taut beneath his touch.

'See?' he taunted softly. 'Your body can't lie. It's naked beneath me in more ways than one. It loves it...'

Grasping her waist, he bent to flick his tongue over the rock-hard nipples, bringing a whimper of dismay from Beth's parted, panting lips. For she could not deny the insidious pleasure that licked along her veins each time this devil's tongue found its mark.

Oh, God...if only he would *stop*!

But not only did he not stop, he went further, drawing each nipple into his mouth in turn, his gentle sucking producing the most deliciously exciting sensations Beth had ever felt. Sensual shivers rippled over her entire skin, a ragged moan of unconscious surrender breaking from her lips.

Uzziah's head lifted, black eyes blazing down at her in wicked triumph. 'You see?' he rasped. 'You want me as much as I want you. Do not fight me any more, my sweet savage. We have no more need of games...'

Bending his head, he planted hotly tempestuous kisses on her mouth, her throat, her collarbones, before returning once more to her breasts, pleasuring them again with his lips and tongue till she was panting with a wild, breathless arousal.

'Such beautiful breasts,' he muttered thickly against her skin. 'Such a beautiful body...' His mouth began to travel down towards her stomach, his tongue trailing a moist path of excitement as it encircled her navel then went down further...

Beth's eyes rounded, for this was what Vernon had wanted to do to her, though she hadn't let him. The very idea had disgusted her. With Uzziah, however, her thighs seemed to be parting of their own accord, her back arching up to press her heated flesh to his hungry lips. She cried out under his gloriously intimate kisses, accepting them readily with an abandoned joy that should have shocked the life out of her, but didn't.

Here she was, bound to a barbarian's bed, theoretically being forced to submit to his demands. But was she struggling, or screaming? No, she was wallowing wantonly in a sea of erotic bliss, thinking that *this* was what she had read about, *this* was what love-making should always be like...

A small gasp escaped when Uzziah's mouth shifted focus slightly, but soon she was moaning softly and wondering if one could die from such pleasure. A sob of sheer ecstasy broke from her lips, tears of happiness flooding her eyes. That miracle she had dreamt of, but never hoped for, was surely going to come about.

Uzziah suddenly abandoned her, rising up to frown down into her tear-stained face.

'Why are you crying?' he demanded to know. 'Did you not like that? Isn't this what you wanted?'

When he lightly touched the bindings around her wrists her cheeks flamed. She had forgotten that he thought her some kind of deviant.

She shook her head violently, her happiness fading as shame and embarrassment reared their ugly heads. 'I want you to untie me,' she cried.

His eyes darkened with exasperation. 'Must you keep lying? I had you mindless with pleasure just now. I have no doubt I could do the same to you again within seconds.'

He ran a taunting hand across the tips of her breasts, making her tremble anew.

'Don't... please don't. Oh, you don't understand. Just now, I admit... I've never felt anything like it. Never ever! But it has nothing to do with being tied up. I actually forgot I *was* till you reminded me.'

His expression was sceptical. 'Then what were the tears for?'

She groaned her frustration. 'I was happy,' she cried. '*Happy*! I've only ever been with one man in my life before and I hated it. For years, I've thought I was frigid! My tears were tears of relief and joy. Please, Uzziah, there's no need to keep me tied up. I won't scratch you again or try to run away. I promise...'

He stared at her for a long time. 'You swear you are telling me the truth?'

'On my mother's grave,' she croaked.

A shadow passed over his face. 'Your mother is dead?'

'Yes,' she whispered, remembered pain in her face. 'My father too.'

His frown deepened. 'You are alone in the world?'

She nodded, then shook her head. 'I do have Pete.'

'Who's Pete? Your brother?'

'No. I have no brothers or sisters. He's a...a friend.'

'But *not* your one and only lover.'

'No!'

Uzziah rolled from her, and Beth shuddered with relief. Now he would untie her.

But he didn't! He simply stretched out beside her, making no move to release her from her bondage. Propping himself up on one elbow, he smiled down at her, his expression one of great satisfaction. 'So, I was right after all. You had a bad experience once which turned you off men and sex. A regrettable occurrence. But never fear... I have already shown you there is nothing to be afraid of and everything to be delighted with. And you have shown me you are a very sensual woman, one who will quickly be aroused again.'

When his mouth began to descend towards her, she squawked her startled shock. 'W...w...what are you doing? Aren't you going to untie me?'

His head retreated, his eyes flashing wickedly down at her. 'We have already established that your being tied up is no barrier to *your* arousal. For my part, I have just discovered I rather like having you at my mercy. It adds a certain piquant pleasure to the proceedings. This way, you have no option but to place yourself in my hands. Believe me... They can be very gentle hands, when they want to be. Trust me...'

Trust him? It was one thing for him to tie her up when she'd been spitting and clawing, when he'd believed she liked it that way, quite another for him to keep her bound *after* she had calmed down and he *knew* it wasn't her idea of fun! It just showed how much of a barbarian he really was. She could not understand why her body responded to him the way it did. He was nothing but a snake!

Her eyes must have told him something of her speechless outrage, for he laughed.

'If only you knew how wildly attractive I find you when you look at me like that. You're like a spirited yearling who refuses to be ridden, who fights the weight in the saddle to the death, ignorant of the knowledge that there is nothing to fear. I will not hurt you, I promise. My only wish is to make beautiful love to you...'

She stared up at him, desperate to say something cutting, anything that would slice into this man's incredible ego. But any hope of speech died when, with palm facing upwards, he trickled his right hand down her body from her shoulder to her stomach, passing over a breast on the way.

Stiffening, she held her breath, hating herself for the way her flesh broke out into goose-bumps, *despising* herself for wanting him to do it again. At last, the breath rushed from her, coming out in a tortured shudder of treacherous pleasure.

'You really like that, don't you?' he murmured, his gaze heavy-lidded upon her as he did it over and over, first her left side then her right, sometimes bypassing her nipples, but mostly not, skimming lightly over the treacherous points which were straining eagerly upwards to meet his touch. They weren't the only parts of her body he teased, for, with each sweep of his hand, he went further and further down towards the V between her thighs, at last brushing the soft blonde curls that guarded her melting womanhood.

When she squeezed her legs tightly together, he responded by abandoning that activity altogether. Her eyes snapped to his before she could stop them.

His returning look was annoyingly bland. 'You want me to keep doing that? No?'

She just glimpsed a hint of a smile before he bent his head.

'No, don't,' she groaned.

Uzziah ignored her protest. He ignored all her protests. And there were many.

Slowly and inexorably he moved her past her futile cries of shocked outrage, past any lingering fears of inadequacy, past any cohesive thought at all. She became a woman stripped of all pretence and inhibition, an excited, ignited sexual being who burnt for his touch, begged for his lips, ached for his possession.

She had a brief moment of being jerked back to reality when he stopped to draw on protection for them both, his action bringing a degree of dismay. For the sensible precaution hadn't even occurred to her. She was far too excited, far too impatient to experience all that Uzziah's body promised. For she knew that what she had felt earlier would be nothing to the pleasure of having her flesh enclose around his in total intimacy.

When he finally moved over and into her, his name fluttered from her lips on a sigh of sheer, sensual pleasure. Vernon had not felt anything like this, she thought dazedly. Vernon she had not felt at all!

Her back arched with voluptuous delight, her hips lifting to take his swollen desire fully within her.

Uzziah groaned, then remained tantalisingly still, his arms reaching up to lie along hers, the weight of his chest squashing her breasts between them. He brushed his mouth over her swollen lips, his tongue tip moistening them.

'Open your mouth,' he commanded softly.

She did, her senses leaping when he slid his tongue inside. Quite automatically, her lips closed around his tongue. When she sucked it gently his whole body shuddered.

Beth was simply stunned by the intoxicating pleasure his response sent rushing through her. Uzziah seemed a little stunned as well, for he lifted his head to stare down into her flushed face with wide black eyes.

'Incredible,' he muttered, and, reaching up, he swiftly untied her, taking her limp arms and placing them around his back. 'I want you to hold me,' he whispered at her lips. 'Touch me, move with me...'

The passion in his voice sent shivers up and down her spine. 'Yes,' she agreed breathlessly, her fingertips pressing deeply into his back as she clasped him to her. Again, he trembled, thrilling her to the depths of her being.

There was no time, however, for her to explore further avenues of this new-found feminine power, for suddenly Uzziah began kissing her with a devastating hunger. Simultaneously, he started to really make love to her, his tongue and body surging in parallel rhythms that were unbelievably exciting.

She responded to his urgency with an instinctive rhythm of her own, her bottom lifting as he thrust deeper and deeper into her eager flesh. There was no thought of trying to stifle her frequent moans, or the escalation of her breathing. Her senses had spiralled out of control into a world where nothing existed but the mad pleasure of it all, where there could be no end but one.

Still, Beth's innocence left her unprepared for the intensity of her climax, her eyes flinging wide when her body started to convulse shamelessly around Uzziah's. She wrenched away from his mouth, his name flying from her lips in a gasping cry of astonishment. His answer was a deep grunt of satisfaction and a quickening of his rhythm, his powerful thrusting soon bringing his own body to an explosive conclusion. His back bowed away from her, his head thrown back, his lips parting wide in a growl of raw release.

When he finally collapsed back upon her, Beth automatically gathered him close, her hands seemingly operating on some instinctive level as she stroked his hair and sighed her own contentment. Eventually, Uzziah rolled over on to his back, taking her with him so that she was stretched out on top of his body. His strong arms moved to wrap tightly around her.

'Fantastic,' he murmured. 'Simply fantastic...'

His words sent a flush of pleasure suffusing through Beth. She lay there, her cheek against his chest, listening to his thudding heartbeat slowly regain a semblance of normality, not sure whose pleasure had thrilled her most. His, or her own. All she knew was that she had never felt so happy as she did at this moment. She didn't want to move. She wanted to stay right where she was, secure in Uzziah's embrace, her memory searching to relive every marvellous moment of what had just happened.

But her satiated body had other ideas. The languorous aftermath of their torrid lovemaking was seeping into her bones, bringing with it a yawn of mental and physical exhaustion.

'Sleep, my darling,' Uzziah crooned, his hands hypnotically soothing as they stroked softly up and down her spine. 'Sleep...'

The last thing she remembered was his easing her down on to cool cushions, then something silky, but surprisingly warm being drawn up over her limp body.

She woke to the lightest of touches on her face, her long lashes flickering open to find Uzziah propped up on his elbow next to her, smiling a sensuous smile while he ran a single fingertip up and down her cheek. She quickly noted that while her own naked body was covered by a pale blue satin quilt, his was lying with blasé nonchalance on top of it. Her response to seeing his magnificent body totally nude again was startling and immediate, her pulse-rate accelerating from a sleep-dazed neutral to a very wide-awake top gear in record time.

'You've been asleep for hours,' he said. 'It'll be dawn soon.'

She stared up at him, the sudden thought insinuating that she probably should be angry with him for doing what he had done last night, manhandling her like that, tying her up then ruthlessly reducing her to a mindlessly sensual creature.

The woman of twenty-four hours ago would have been furious.

But she wasn't that woman any more. All she felt when she looked upon his admittedly arrogant but extremely handsome face was joy and gratitude. He had found the woman in her, brought it to the surface, set her soul free of bitterness and cynicism. He had shown her what making love *could* be like. She would remember him till her dying day with warmth and gratitude. And, yes...liking. Aisha had been right about that. She did like Uzziah. Maybe too much.

It would not be wise, she realised, to fall in love with such a man.

'Don't frown,' he murmured, and bent to kiss the puckers on her forehead.

Beth stiffened at the electric charge his lips sparked through her body. Goodness, but a girl could get addicted to this, she thought with a degree of worry. Exultant as she was over at last feeling good about her sexuality, Beth sensed how easily these new desires could get out of hand. She had enjoyed Uzziah's lovemaking—he was clearly an expert—and she would undoubtedly let him do it again before this weekend was up. But she didn't want to make a fool of herself.

'I...I think I would like a shower,' she said, trying to give herself some breathing space from the feelings his naked body were evoking in her. Already her stomach was in knots, and her face, she was sure, had to be flushed.

'My thoughts exactly,' he agreed with a seductive curve to his lips. 'Although I prefer to bathe. I've got it all ready for us.' He climbed off the bed, throwing back the satin quilt and offering her an outstretched hand. 'Come on...'

Flustered at being so smoothly outmanoeuvred, she glanced around for something to put on. His laugh was amused as he took her fluttering hands and drew her to her feet. 'You won't be needing any clothes.' And, scooping her up into his arms again, he began carrying her across the huge room. 'If I have my way you won't be covering up this gorgeous body of yours for the next thirty-six hours.'

Beth blinked up at him. *Gorgeous*? Her once too fat and still too tall, heavy-breasted, wide-hipped, solid-thighed body?

'Yes, gorgeous,' he whispered huskily, and kissed her startled mouth. 'First time I've lain with a woman whom I wasn't afraid I might squash.'

CHAPTER ELEVEN

UZZIAH'S bathroom was a superb example of sheer opulence and decadence. As large as a ballroom, it boasted acres of marble floor; a sunken spa bath that could have doubled as a swimming-pool; a small gym; a massage table; a shower built for six; a triple-basined vanity area; and so many mirrors that Beth could see never-ending reflections of herself.

She was greatly relieved when Uzziah lowered her naked form into the blissfully warm waters and released her to swim away from his overpowering physical presence.

Still not at ease with the stunning effect even the slightest of Uzziah's caresses could have on her, Beth fled to the spa area of the Roman-style bath where jets of foaming water were spurting out from the blue-tiled walls. Finding a ledge below the water, she sat, pretending to luxuriate in the feel of the surging water while she tried to regather her composure.

Fortunately, Uzziah stayed at the other end of the bath, stroking lazily in the water for a while, then leaning back against the wall, his arms outstretched on the tiles. She pretended to ignore his lazy-eyed scrutiny, though her heart was racing madly at the feel of his gaze upon her. His blessed silence, however, gave her room for thought, and a puzzling question slipped into her mind.

Why him? she mused. Why not Vernon?

Vernon was very good-looking and an experienced lover. He had tried to turn her on, but the more he'd touched her the colder she had become. In the end, he'd lost patience with her and simply gone ahead, uncaring if he hurt her. Yet oddly enough he hadn't, not in any physical sense, Beth hardly being aware of his body inside hers. Admittedly, there was one area where he didn't compare favourably with Uzziah, but surely it didn't come down to *that*, did it?

No, no, she dismissed logically. Uzziah had had her trembling with desire well before actual intercourse had come into it.

She glanced up, true confusion in her eyes, only to meet two penetrating black eyes coming steadily closer as he swam towards her.

'You're frowning again,' he said, and abruptly stood up, slicking the long black waves back from his face, the action sending water cascading from his elbows. By the time his hands finally dropped back to his sides, Beth was staring at him with open admiration and desire.

He was so beautiful, she thought with throat drying and heart pounding. So damned beautiful . . .

Her gaze raked over his unusual face, marvelling anew at its exotically sculptured cheekbones; the magnetic, deeply set eyes; the wide, uncompromising mouth. Her insides tensed as she suddenly thought of the sensations that mouth could produce.

Swallowing convulsively, she let her gaze drift down past the aggressive set of his squared chin to the well-proportioned frame of his powerful body, and the superbly honed flesh that covered it. Finally her eyes dropped to the smattering of dark curls that disappeared into the water on its journey down to his loins.

Beth did not have to see his sex to know what it looked like. A man among men, Omar had said. He was not wrong there.

A shiver rippled over her skin, breaking it out into goose-bumps. Beth felt some alarm that even looking at this man could turn her on so. Was she about to become some kind of wanton woman, enslaved by the pleasures of the flesh? She hoped not. She really did.

'You can't be cold,' he said with a seductive smile in his voice.

'Not at all,' she denied, almost laughing at such irony. Couldn't he see that she was on fire for him, that if he touched her now she would go up in flames? 'Probably someone walking over my grave,' she said in a voice so cool she hardly believed it was hers.

He stared at her for several seconds before turning away, thankfully not seeing her expel a great, ragged sigh of relief. Sinking back down into the water's warmth, he breast-stroked over to the adjacent corner where he too sat down on the underwater ledge, stretching his long arms out along the tiles in an attitude of enviable relaxation. His gaze was impassive when it returned to her.

'Tell me some more about yourself. When did your parents die and who is this Pete you spoke of?'

Beth was only too happy to talk, if it kept him at arm's length for a while. She needed time to collect herself, to become accustomed to this new self who only had to *look* at this man to be stirred by needs she had to fight to control.

So she told him everything about herself, from the time her mother died of cancer when she was eight, to her father's slowly drinking himself to death during the years afterwards while she ate her grief-stricken self into an unhappy, overweight teenager. She revealed things about those wretched years that she had never told anyone, even Pete, especially how crushed she had been when as well as being far too plump she had started growing taller and taller, well past all the boys in her class.

'I wasn't grossly fat,' she admitted. 'I did too much exercise for that. But compared to the other girls, I felt enormous. Perhaps if I'd had a pretty face——'

Uzziah's scoffing sound had her eyes snapping to his in sudden anger. 'If you say I'm pretty, I'll... I'll——'

'I won't,' he cut in with brutal honesty. 'But who wants pretty? You have good bones in your face. It has character and class. You will be a fine-looking woman when all the pretty faces are shrivelled up old hags!'

Tears pricked at her eyes, her heart squeezing tight. She threw him a slightly sardonic smile. 'Do you always know just what to say to women?'

His frown showed she had hit a nerve with this remark. 'I wouldn't have thought so. I haven't made a practice of flattery. I haven't needed to...' He stared at her for a long moment before continuing. 'Tell me more about your schooldays. What was the worst thing that happened to you during those years? The one memory that hurts the most.'

'That's easy,' she told him with a brittle laugh. 'It was every time the school held a disco. God, but I hated hearing the girls at school on those days, happily planning what they would wear that night, giggling over what boys might be there...

'I never went, of course. I stayed home and stuffed myself with chocolates and lollies, after which I would go to bed and cry myself to sleep. If I hadn't had my horses,' she finished with a catch in her voice, 'I don't know what I would have done.'

'I can appreciate that. Horses make great companions. Like all animals, they love you for your inner self, not for what you look like, or who your parents were, or even what you own.'

The unexpected bitterness in *his* voice reached out to Beth, moving her. She was startled, then intrigued, by the range of emotions this man could evoke in her. Who would ever believe that this self-contained and very strong man could have been so deeply hurt by other people? Yet clearly, he had...

'Go on,' he said brusquely, seeing her curious glance. 'Tell me how you came to be running this riding school you spoke of.'

She cleared her throat, then launched into a concise, and hopefully less emotional recounting of how, after her father's death, she had left school early to try to resurrect the riding school her mother had first started and which her drunken father had almost ruined. She even told him about the riding lessons she gave once every month to handicapped children.

'You've no idea how much those poor kids enjoy their time with the horses. Their eyes light up with real happiness, especially the spastic ones. Suddenly, they're mobile without having to look uncoordinated and awkward.'

'A nice change, I suppose,' Uzziah said ruefully, 'from being stared and laughed at. If there's anything that gets me riled it's the way supposedly civilised folk look askance at anyone who's just a wee bit different, who simply doesn't fit into their idea of the norm!'

More than a *little* riled, I'd say, Beth decided when she noted Uzziah's suddenly clenched fists and angry scowl. She certainly wouldn't like to get on the wrong side of *his* temper, that was for sure. There again, she would also like to have him batting in her corner if she was in trouble, or danger.

Suddenly, Omar's claim that Uzziah had once saved his life popped into her mind.

'Now can I ask *you* something?' she said. 'If you promise not to get mad, that is.'

He looked taken aback. 'Why should I get mad?'

'I'm not sure... It's just that Omar seemed to think that——'

'Omar?' he cut in, the scowl back. 'What has that infernal man been saying about me now? He should attend to his own shortcomings, not go round expounding mine.'

'He wasn't expounding any such thing,' Beth defended. 'He mentioned, however, that you had this aversion to women being told anything about you on a personal level.'

'And rightly so, too,' he muttered. 'Tell a woman anything and she will eventually try to use it against you.'

'I doubt that applies to me, Uzziah,' she said crisply, 'since I will be gone from your life on Monday.'

His frown was dark and disgruntled. Clearly, he did not like being on the end of either questions or challenging remarks, but Beth refused to back down this time. She was too curious.

'Omar said that you had once saved his life and I was wondering exactly how that came about.'

Uzziah's laughter startled her. 'Saved his life? Good lord, what an incorrigible exaggerater that man is!

Saved his life!' He chuckled again. 'Now that's a good one. Still, some people might say that I rescued him from a fate worse than death, though I find that questionable. Nothing compares with the devastation death can bring.'

Once again, a wealth of bitterness swept across his handsome features. Beth was wide-eyed with speculation, wondering whose death had touched Uzziah's soul so deeply and tragically. But, just as quickly, his face cleared of any distress, his dark eyes unreadable as they sought hers.

'I have digressed,' he apologised smoothly. 'Back to my moment of glory. Omar and I were sent to the same school as young lads, a very privileged school in the south of England. Omar's father, you see, was an extremely wealthy Moroccan merchant who thought an English education was essential for his very bright second son. Unfortunately, Omar was small for his age. This, plus his dark skin and rather effeminate features, made him the target of a certain element in the school. I discovered him two days after we arrived, about to be... *initiated* ... by a couple of the older students.'

One of his eyebrows lifted sardonically. 'You get my drift?'

She nodded, her mouth dry.

'Being somewhat averse to unprovoked violence of any kind, I immediately stepped into the fray, proclaiming myself Omar's champion in the time-honoured English tradition of knighthood. Luckily, I was a well-grown lad, as well as having been taught how to defend myself from early childhood. The bedouins, you see, are warriors. I must say I gave a good account of myself, though my solicitor was not

impressed with the medical bills and damages he had
to settle at a later date to keep me out of court. Omar
was suitably grateful and followed me round like a
little puppy for the rest of our school years, which
unfortunately gave rise to rumours about our relationship which I was occasionally forced to rectify.'

Beth had no trouble imagining exactly how this rec-
tifying was achieved.

'Still,' Uzziah went on carelessly, 'I have been
suitably repaid for my gallantry. When Omar went on
to gain honours in a business degree, I hired him as
my personal secretary and financial adviser. I must
say he is a particularly loyal employee with a sheer
genius for investment, though his tendency to be in-
gratiating in public is a trifle irritating at times.'

'You mean it's not your idea that he calls you
master?'

'Good God, no. He enjoys the looks of wide-eyed
speculation that his unctuous servitude brings from
my guests and business acquaintances. The man's
wickedly devious to the core. Which reminds me, I
must speak to him again about a certain matter, make
sure he does the right thing...

'But enough of talk about *my* past, it's yours I'm
trying to find out about. Tell me where this Pete comes
into things?'

Beth sighed, dying to know more of Uzziah's background but aware that she had no hope of getting
more out of him right now. She was forced to satisfy
his curiosity, while squashing her own.

Pete, she explained patiently, was the invalid pen-
sioner cook-cum-housekeeper she'd employed shortly
after her father died, simply because he was the only
applicant she could afford. He had offered himself

for no salary for the first six months, in exchange for room and board. They had got along immediately, both no-nonsense people with a similar dry sense of humour. A returned soldier who had never married, Pete seemed to find in Beth the daughter he never had, always giving her the pearls of his wisdom through cynical sayings such as his now ironically infamous 'There's no such thing as a sure thing.'

'Sounds like a wise man,' Uzziah drawled with a twinkle in his eye.

'Yes, well I wouldn't be here now, would I, if I'd listened to him?'

'Wouldn't you?' Uzziah said, his voice dropping to a low, sensual whisper.

Beth's heart stopped as their eyes met.

He surged towards her through the water, his large hands reaching out to span her waist, drawing her from the ledge and hard against him. Her pulse raced as she realised his desire had been well and truly renewed. Hers, she conceded, had never really abated.

'You would have been mine,' he insisted thickly, 'lost race or not.'

His arrogance took her breath away. Yet it was his very arrogance she found insidiously attractive. Beth accepted somewhat dazedly that there was an elemental weakness in women that responded to this brand of raw masculinity. Even while her mind was repelled by the thought of any man dominating her so completely, her female body floundered beneath Uzziah's masterful ways.

Still, the remnants of her pride compelled her to try to rock that smug confidence of his. 'How can you be so sure of that?' she challenged.

He smiled. 'Simple. I knew the moment I lifted you down from that helicopter that you wanted me as much as I wanted you.'

'Don't be ridiculous!' she snapped. 'That's just not true!'

'It most certainly *was* true.'

'Rubbish! I wasn't even remotely thinking about sex when I arrived here. All I was thinking about was your horses! It was your colt I coveted, not you!'

'Your mind was thinking about horses,' he insisted with maddening certainty. 'Your body was thinking about sex.'

Beth fell silent, remembering how she hadn't been able to take her eyes off him, how she had kept pulling away from his touch as if he was electrified. So it was as simple as that, was it? One person's body chemistry sparking off another's. How many men were there in this world, she wondered, to whom she could respond as she had to Uzziah? Two? Fifty? A hundred?

Her heart contracted. Funny... She didn't like to think there could be so many. She didn't like to think there could be *any*! She only wanted to want *this* man, not any others. He was her one and only real lover, the special discoverer of her most intimate secrets. He and he alone had seen her eyes widen at the moment of orgasm, had heard her intimate moans of pleasure, had felt her flesh squeezing tight with ecstasy. To be like that with another man was unthinkable!

'I hate it when you frown like that,' he gruffed.

She glanced up into his broodingly handsome face and told herself not to be such a naïve, romantic fool. Uzziah had had a host of women moaning under him. Beth Carney was nothing special. So why should she bestow such a special tag on him? It was foolish and self-destructive. She had to keep thinking of him as nothing more than a holiday affair, an erotic adventure, a wild fling; for come Tuesday she'd be on a flight back to Australia, never to see him again.

Common sense had spoken!

Why, then, Beth agonised, did she suddenly feel so wretched?

'I want to see a smile,' he insisted testily.

It took considerable effort for her to find one, but, once she had, she did feel better. Especially when he smiled back at her.

'Now put your arms around my neck,' he ordered, 'and tell me how that bastard of a neighbour of yours managed to get past your defences. No lies now! I want the unvarnished truth.'

With some reluctance Beth managed to tell the tale of her weight loss five years ago and Vernon's one-night interest in her, including his callous dismissal the morning after.

'What a selfish pig,' Uzziah pronounced at her conclusion, then lanced her with a reproachful look. 'But how on earth could you possibly have concluded that every future sexual encounter would be a non-event for you, just because your first one was? I would have thought you'd have had more intelligence!'

'Intelligence doesn't come into it, Uzziah, when you've felt unattractive all your life and expected nothing from the opposite sex but scorn and revulsion. Even after I slimmed down, I still didn't feel attractive. Men didn't seem to find me attractive either.'

'What rubbish! You're very attractive, with an incredibly sexy body. You can't tell me you haven't been on the receiving end of male desire every now and then over the past five years.'

She flushed guiltily, remembering the occasions she had been approached by men down at the pub, only to reject their advances with castrating looks and caustic comments.

'I guess I just wasn't receptive,' she admitted slowly. 'Maybe I was still hurting from all those years of being unloved and unwanted. Even my father used to tell me I should have been born a boy, that I wasn't at all feminine or desirable.'

Uzziah looked deep into her eyes, his glittering black gaze showing how much *he* desired her. Not that she didn't know that already. She could feel the evidence brushing against her thighs.

'Now you know how wrong you were, don't you?' he murmured, cupping her face and kissing her with infinite sweetness. 'I wanted you more than any woman I've ever met. Why do you think I wouldn't let you go back to Cairo, why I contrived that one-sided bet? I was mad for you. Simply mad . . .'

She trembled underneath his hungry kiss.

'We're going to go back to bed now,' he said in that thickened tone she adored. 'And you're going to make love to me.'

'Am I?' She stared up into his heavy-lidded eyes, her head spinning.

'Just say yes to everything.'

She nodded, her mouth dry.

'You're going to be on top.'

She swallowed.

'You're going to drive me wild.'

She shuddered as he took her mouth once more.

CHAPTER TWELVE

'IT MUST be very late,' Beth said.

'Does it matter? We can stay in bed all day if we want to. If you're hungry I can have a tray sent in.'

'Oh, no, don't do that,' she said hurriedly. 'I . . . I'd be embarrassed.'

Uzziah's laugh was warm as he pulled her back more tightly into him, spoon fashion. He kissed her first on the ear-lobe, then on her neck and shoulder, his hands sliding up over her ribs to fondle her breasts. Beth was astounded to feel her breath quickening again.

'Uzziah, this is crazy. We can't do it again. I . . . I'll . . .'

'You'll what?' he whispered into her ear.

Any further argument was interrupted by a knocking at the main doors in the living-room. It sounded like a code. Tap-tap; tap-tap-tap; tap-tap.

'Damn,' Uzziah muttered.

'Who is it?' Beth asked.

'Omar.'

'What do you think he wants?'

'Me, I'm afraid. I've just remembered today's the first Sunday of the month.'

'And?'

'I hold a type of people's court on the first Sunday of every month. Look, I'll go and tell Omar I'll be with him shortly. You stay put!' he ordered her, throwing back the covers and leaping, naked, to his feet. Scooping up his black robe, he dropped it over his head and hurried from the room.

A people's court?

Beth waited impatiently for his return, her curiosity aroused. Luckily, she didn't have to wait for long, Uzziah striding back with a scowl on his handsome face. 'It seems I have a long line of disgruntled people this month,' he said by way of explanation, before heading for the bathroom. 'I'll try to be as quick as I can,' he threw back over his shoulder.

The sound of the shower going warned her not to attempt any further long-distance conversation. Uzziah emerged after a few minutes, garbed in a long, snow-white linen robe, tan sandals on his feet, his wet black waves slicked back and secured in a knot at the nape of his neck.

'I'll try not to be too long,' he said apologetically.

'Can't I come and watch?'

He laughed his surprise. 'What on earth for? It's deadly dull. Just me playing Solomon over a lot of petty little squabbles.'

'I would *like* to see you playing Solomon.'

He frowned at her. 'You are a strange female. Any other woman would much rather lie in bed there and be pampered. I was about to send Aisha along with a breakfast tray for you.'

'I'd rather eat later,' she said. 'With you.'

He stared at her for a prolonged moment.

'You may come if you promise to stay in the background. And not say a single word!'

Beth was inconspicuous, leaning against one of the many marble columns, almost as fascinated by her surroundings as by the proceedings. For Uzziah's court was being conducted in the ballroom with its sleek black marble floor underfoot and splendid stained-glass dome overhead. Uzziah himself sat on a large, throne-like chair at one end of the room, the various petitioners lined up before him in a very long file. Omar stood on his master's right-hand side, relaying each problem out loud in his pompous-sounding voice. Unfortunately, not in English.

Uzziah seemed a very decisive judge, however, because he didn't ask too many questions, just listened to the person, or to both people if that was the case, then made his pronouncement. Whatever he said seemed to be very well accepted, as though everyone knew he was a fair and just judge.

Only once did a man raise his voice in protest, and he was the last in the line. Whatever he said had an immediate effect. Uzziah jumped to his feet, shouting something in Arabic and pointing angrily to the double doors at the back of the ballroom. The man cried out in anguish, dropping to Uzziah's feet and kissing them over and over. Uzziah sighed, then sat down and laid his hand softly on the young man's head in a gesture of forgiveness, whereupon the suppliant lifted his head, beaming his relief.

The interchange affected Beth, tears pricking at her eyes. She blinked them away, surprised at herself. But then she saw that the incident echoed her own situation. She, too, would be sent away soon, banished from Uzziah's *domaine* as surely as this man had been about to be banished. Uzziah had no permanent need of any woman. He did not fall in love. He did not marry. He simply entertained . . . guests.

If she were to throw herself at his feet and beg him to let her stay, would he be moved to mercy as he had been just now? She doubted it, doubted it very much.

A sudden commotion at the back of the room distracted her from the feeling of intense bleakness her thoughts had evoked.

'Don't be ridiculous!' a woman's voice was saying haughtily as the double doors were flung open. 'Of course I can come in here. I am Uzziah's mother, young lady!'

Uzziah's *mother*?

Beth blinked, then stared as an extremely tall, grey-haired woman in a navy blue gabardine suit launched her way across the marble floor, Aisha trailing after her with an anxious look on her face.

'Uzziah!' the elderly woman commanded as she marched forward. 'Tell this servant girl who I am! She must be relatively new around here since she didn't recognise me.'

Uzziah rose slowly to his feet, a closed expression on his face. He turned to speak briefly to Omar, who nodded and left the room, taking the young man and Aisha with him. The double doors shut with a clang, leaving Uzziah alone with his mother.

Or so she might have thought. Beth wondered if even Uzziah had forgotten she was there.

'Aisha has been in my employ for over a year, Mother,' Uzziah informed in a silky drawl which Beth suspected covered a wealth of irritation. 'May I ask what has brought about this unexpected visit? After the last occasion, I rather expected you would not return here.'

She waved a dismissive hand. 'I had a very good reason.'

'Another worthy cause?' he said drily. 'What is it this time? Another home for teenage runaways? You could have wired for the money, you know, Mother. It would have been a lot cheaper than coming all this way, even if you did use *my* helicopter.'

The woman lifted her chin. 'I came in on your weekly supply flight and I paid for my own flight from London. Does it not ever occur to you, Uzziah, that I might want to see you for reasons other than money?'

'No,' he pronounced coldly. 'So just tell me how much you need. A couple of hundred thousand? Half a million? What will it take to get you back on that helicopter and out of here in less than half an hour?'

Now it was Beth's turn to gasp, the startled sound echoing in the cavernous room. The woman whirled, spotting her immediately. Steely grey eyes narrowed on to Beth's long fair hair, which was flowing in erotic disarray down over Uzziah's black robe. Beth cringed inside, regretting her decision to cover her nakedness with the first thing that had come to hand.

'So!' the elderly woman sneered, her thin lips curling with disdain as she folded her arms. '*This* is why you want me out of here so quickly. You have one of your shameless hussies staying with you!'

Beth's mouth gaped with shock at such rudeness. Her eyes flew to Uzziah, who was looking as if he could quietly kill his mother.

'That's enough,' he ground out, a dull, angry red suffusing his high cheekbones. 'You will not spout your hypocritical religious scruples in my home, do you hear me? A woman giving herself to a man with warmth and affection is not shameless. Neither does it make her a hussy.'

'Then what does it make her?' his mother retorted tartly. 'A saint?'

'Perhaps.'

'A slut, more like it!'

'Only in your sick mind,' he countered savagely. 'I'll have you know that Beth happens to be the most genuine, loving, caring, wonderful woman it has ever been my good fortune to meet! I am privileged to have had the honour to just know her, let alone been fortunate enough to experience the comfort of her lovely body. I only hope that I will be able to repair the harm you have just done with your sour-graped tongue. What a pity you weren't forced to stay in my father's bed a little longer! Maybe with enough time he might have been able to break through that concrete cast you wear around your heart in the name of virtue!'

Beth was flattered by Uzziah's compliments to herself, but *appalled* by the brutal attack on his mother. Could he not see all the blood drain from her face? Or the haunted look his words had brought to her eyes?

No, she realised, glancing at his coldly furious face. He could see nothing through his own anger.

Yet it was simply awful having to stand there silently and watch him tear strips off his mother like that. The woman was probably as narrow-minded and self-righteous as he was saying. But she was also quite old—seventy at least—and no doubt a victim of the kind of strict religious upbringing very common to her time.

Hadn't Monsieur Renault said she'd been a missionary when she was kidnapped and given to Uzziah's father? If that was so, then the experience of being taken by force when she was probably a not-so-young virgin would have been horrendous! Beth was not surprised that the old lady's views on sex were tainted. It was a pity Uzziah could not be more understanding and forgiving.

'Uzziah!' Beth began in a voice of such uncompromising firmness that his eyes jerked round to stare at her. 'This is not the time or the place to talk of these things. They are private and personal. Surely you can see that you have upset your mother terribly. Or don't you care? If you don't, then you are not the man I thought you were!'

She came forwards to gently take the pale-faced woman by the arm. 'Come, I will take you to my room while your son finds his manners. Uzziah, would you please have a tea tray sent along? Then, afterwards, when you are feeling more like yourself, you might like to join us.'

She gave his shocked face one last reproachful glance before leading his equally stunned mother away.

'My name is Beth,' she said as soon as they had turned a corner and Uzziah was out of sight. 'And if you're wondering about the accent, I'm from Australia. And what shall I call you?'

The old lady stopped and blinked at her. 'I... Irene.'

'Irene.' Beth smiled and patted the old lady's hand. 'Now don't you go letting Uzziah worry you, Irene. He's a bit of a bully and was just letting off steam. Of course, as his mother, you should understand that he's a grown man now and can live his life as he pleases. You might not agree with some of the things he does, but you really shouldn't say so, you know. Not if you want to remain on good terms with him.'

When they resumed walking, Beth tripped on the hem of the black robe, which was far too long for her. It reminded her of her naked state underneath, reminded her of what Uzziah's mother had called her.

'I do want you to know, Irene,' she explained once they arrived at the door to the guest quarters, 'that I am not in the habit of spending the night with a man. But your son, Uzziah . . . well . . . he is the first man to make me feel the way I felt last night and I can only say that——'

Beth never got any further. For Uzziah's mother burst into tears, noisy wretched sobs racking her body as she buried her face in her hands.

Beth didn't know what to do. In the end, she bustled the distressed old lady inside, settling her on one of the small sofas before hurrying to retrieve a box of tissues from the bathroom. But, on seeing the wretched, huddled figure with its shoulders shaking, she could do nothing else but sit down and take the poor woman in her arms, cradling her firmly against her chest and praying for further inspiration. Fortunately, Aisha's arrival with the tray of tea had Irene swiftly composing herself with the typical Englishwoman's distaste for showing emotion in public.

'Thank you, Aisha,' Beth said as the girl placed the tray on the coffee-table. 'Please tell Sidi Uzziah that his mother is feeling better now and we will expect him to join us in due time.'

Aisha, the little diplomat, made no comment. She merely nodded, then departed. Beth broke the sudden awkward silence by pouring tea and saying, 'At least it's English tea, and not mint. Do you like milk and sugar, Irene?'

The old lady managed a shaky nod. 'You're so kind,' she murmured brokenly. 'I . . . I don't deserve it.'

'Why ever not?'

Irene lifted startled grey eyes.

'What have you ever done that was so wrong,' Beth went on, 'but love and care for your son under what I imagine were very difficult circumstances? I know how Uzziah came to be conceived and I assure you, Irene, you have my full understanding in the matter.'

The old lady slowly shook her head. 'No . . . you don't understand. The nights I spent with Uzziah's father. They were . . . were . . .'

'Dreadful, I'm sure,' Beth finished for her.

'No,' came the shaky denial. 'They were w . . . wonderful . . .'

Beth's eyes blinked wide, but she said nothing.

'You . . . you can't know what it was like. There I was, a dried-up old spinster of forty who'd never been looked at by a man in all her life. I was far too plain, too tall, too plump. And suddenly, there I was, propelled into the harem of an Arab sheikh who was so handsome that any woman would have swooned. Not only that, he was so kind about it all, so . . . gallant. He sat me down that first night and explained that he had to take me to bed, or bring dishonour to the tribe who gave me to him as a gift, but that he would be gentle . . .

'From the first moment he touched me, I was . . . bewitched. I tried not to show it. I tried to resist. But I failed . . . I failed . . .' Irene let out a ragged sigh, her eyes filling with tears again. 'I was so ashamed the next morning. So horribly ashamed.'

She looked up at Beth, her brimming eyes pleading for understanding. Little did she know that Beth, more than anyone, could understand exactly what had happened.

'I vowed never to let him touch me again. But the next night, when he sent for me, I was so...*flattered*...that he would want me a second time that I just melted. I think I fell in love with Rachid that night. No, I don't think so. I know I did. But at the same time, I hated him for being able to make me feel and do things I thought were wickedly wrong.'

'But they weren't wrong,' Beth pointed out gently. 'Surely you can see that now?'

'Yes . . . yes, I think perhaps I finally do. The truth hit me when you told me about the way Uzziah made *you* feel. Yet you're such a good girl. I can see that. But it's awfully hard to put aside what's been ingrained into your mind since childhood. Sex without marriage was taboo in my family. Having not only indulged, but indulged with pleasure, I was filled with remorse. When I found out I was pregnant I was so stricken with guilt and despair that my love turned to hate.'

Her sigh was a deep, emotional shudder. 'This time I did refuse to let Rachid touch me again. He had previously promised to let me go after a couple of months, but now he forced me to stay until Uzziah was born in case I did something silly. Not that I would have. That would have been an even greater crime in my eyes than what I had already done.'

'So you were finally allowed to take Uzziah back to England with you?'

'Yes. Though Rachid had no intention of letting his son go completely. He insisted the boy spend a part of each year with him. When I refused the first time, he had Uzziah kidnapped. I have never known such grief and torment! By the time my baby was returned several weeks later I agreed to do as Rachid asked from that moment, so the boy was shared between us.'

'Well, that was only sensible, wasn't it?'

Irene shivered. 'I didn't handle it well. Poor Uzziah...he suffered during those growing-up years...being torn this way and that between two different cultures, two different religions. I knew how much he loved his father and yet I kept trying to poison his young mind against Rachid. Not very Christian of me, was it? His father wasn't much better, always telling Uzziah that I had never really loved and wanted him as *he* loved and wanted him. He used to mock my religious beliefs, then shove his own ways down the boy's throat, doing everything he could to corrupt my son away from *my* values. Do you know he was given a woman for his thirteenth birthday? A very experienced woman who showed him everything, taught him everything.'

Beth shook her head, her eyes wide. It was no wonder he was so good at it, she thought wryly. He'd had the right tuition from the word go.

Irene sighed. 'Of course, when he came home and boasted about this I was furious. I took him back with me to confront his father. We were on our way when it happened.'

'When what happened?'

'Rachid and all his family were killed by a bomb.'

'Oh, my God, how awful! But who...why?'

Irene shrugged. 'Terrorists. We never found out which group exactly. Rachid was not popular among some of his people. He was considered too liberal in his views. And too friendly with the West.'

'Poor Uzziah,' Beth murmured.

'Yes, he was most distraught. Not only was his father killed, but so were his half-brothers and sisters and their mothers. The only people left from the Arab side of his life was a certain bedouin tribe he was close to. It was from them he learnt his love of horses. He still insisted he spend some time every year with them, and I did not have the heart to refuse. Though I suspect if I did, he would have found a way to go without my permission. Suddenly, at thirteen, he was a very rich, amazingly grown-up, extremely cynical young man. The money his father had left him, he once told me, would eventually give him the power to step away from this world, to hold it in the contempt it deserved.'

'Oh, dear,' Beth said sadly.

'Yes,' Irene concurred. 'Uzziah had become hard. But I lived in hope that he would change, that the years would soften his heart. Only once were my hopes raised. There was this girl at the time, a rich English girl he was in love with. But her family, it seemed, wouldn't have an illegitimate half-breed for a son-in-law, and the girl would not go against their wishes. After that, Uzziah became even more cynical. He spent more and more time here. And he had lots of different women. All of a similar type. Shallow and fast. I had to accept in the end that he had no intention of ever getting married or having children of his own. Perhaps I am to blame for that. I have not been a good mother. I have not set a good example.'

'Don't judge yourself so harshly,' Beth soothed. 'Uzziah may be a touch cynical about women and marriage, but he is still a fine man. A good man. You can be proud of him. I understand that you might be disappointed with some aspects of his life, but, as an adult, he has the right to live his life as he sees fit. Let him be and love him anyway.'

'But I do!' Irene insisted. 'I love him to death.'

'Then don't lecture. You cannot change him anyway. That I have already learnt in a very short time. Who knows? Maybe...one day...he will choose to change himself.'

Irene stared at her. 'How can it be that you are so young, yet so wise?'

'I'm not so young,' Beth said wryly. 'Neither am I so wise. But I know your son. Not just biblically speaking,' she added with a small smile. 'He has more of your moral strength and character than you realise, though, like you, he can be stubborn and rigid in his thinking. But he is held in high regard by the people who work for him. They respect him; admire him; *trust* him. I have also seen him handle a newborn foal with a touch so gentle it would bring tears to your eyes. You have not done too badly in raising your son, Irene. Not too badly at all...'

'If only he would fall in love with girl like you,' the old lady whispered with a deep sincerity.

Beth's heart squeezed tight. 'If only,' she repeated, then brought herself up with a jolt. Oh, no, she realised with a degree of shock. Oh, no...

The truth slotted into place like the last piece in a jigsaw puzzle. *That* was why she had responded so totally to Uzziah, and not at all to Vernon. That was why the thought of leaving here filled her with such a bleak emptiness. Because she had fallen in love.

Irene was staring at her. 'You love him, don't you?'

Beth was about to deny it when she brought herself up short. Why *should* she deny it? She had waited all her life to fall in love. 'With all my heart,' she confessed, a lump in her throat.

There was a sharp rap on the door.

Beth swallowed. 'That will probably be Uzziah.'

'What . . . what will I say to him?' his mother asked in a panic.

'I think you might start by telling him everything you've just told me.'

'Yes . . .' she said slowly, then nodded. 'Yes, I think I will. And you, my dear? Will you tell him that you love him?'

Beth shook her head, her eyes sad. 'I don't think that would be a good idea. I'm leaving here tomorrow. By Tuesday, I'll be winging my way back to Australia.'

CHAPTER THIRTEEN

BUT Tuesday did not find Beth winging her way back to Australia. It found her on the telephone to her home in Galston Gorge.

'Carney's Ridin' School,' Pete answered in his gruff, gravelly voice. 'Pete speakin'.'

'Pete, it's Beth.'

'Beth! How are you, love? I thought it might be you when that foreigner came on the phone. What's up? Your plane been delayed?'

'No. I've just decided to extend my holiday a bit, that's all.'

'You 'aven't found your dream stallion yet?'

The irony of that statement sent a fierce blush to her cheeks.

'No—er—not yet,' she replied, also astonished at how little she had thought about horses the last day or so. 'But I've got the opportunity to stay an extra week at this Arabian horse stud in Morocco,' she raced on nervously. 'Fact is, I'm there now.'

'Morocco?' Pete said, a frown in his voice. 'But that's the other side of Africa, isn't it? 'Ow on earth could you afford to fly over there? I thought you only had just enough money for a week in Egypt.'

'Well actually, it didn't cost me any money, Pete. I'm a guest, you see, and——'

'Now, Beth,' he cut in bluntly. 'There's no such thing as a free lunch. You know that as well as I do.'

'Yes, Pete,' she said with a sigh. 'I know that.'

'Beth? You don't sound like yourself. I think you'd better tell old Pete what's going on. Are you in some sort of trouble?'

'Good heavens, no,' she denied, determined to put Pete's mind at rest. 'I had this chance to look over some really top horses and I just couldn't pass up the opportunity. I did the owner a sort of favour and——'

'What sort of favour?' Pete demanded, clearly not at all mollified.

'I did some riding for him. Put a stroppy black colt over some jumps so well that they sold it for a mint. The owner was ever so grateful.'

'Humph! Those rich owner types are a lot of jet-settin', womanisin' bastards. You watch yourself, my girl. They're not adverse to beddin' the stable-girls, you know.'

'Now, Pete,' she laughed shakily. 'Can you honestly see that type of man getting to first base with me?'

'Why not? Vernon did.'

'Pete!'

'You think I don't know about that? I saw it in your face, love, the very next day. It took all of my control not to go over and knock the bugger's block off. The only thing that stopped me was that by doin' that you'd know I knew. And I figured you needed a little time to get over the hurt.'

'Oh, Pete...' Her eyes began to swim.

'I wouldn't like to see you hurtin' like that again, love. So you be careful, 'ere?'

'Yes, Pete.' Thank God he couldn't see the streams running down her face.

*   *   *

Beth hung up a minute or so later, after Pete re-assured her he could cope alone for another week. Sitting down on the side of the bed, she tried to re-assure *herself* that she wasn't acting like a fool, ac-cepting Uzziah's very casual offer yesterday that she stay a few more days.

There had been nothing casual about what he'd been doing at the time. She'd looked up at him, her pounding heart having stopped midstream.

'You . . . you do pick your moments . . .'

His smile was wicked. 'You'd like to take a short respite to consider?'

'If you stop now I'll strangle you.'

'Then say yes quickly,' he'd rasped with a sudden, passionate urgency.

'Yes,' she'd choked out. 'God, yes . . .'

Beth hung her head in her hands in dismay as she realised she was putty in Uzziah's hands, especially once he started making love to her. Sometimes, she bitterly resented her love for him, especially the way it undermined her will-power. A couple of times over the past two days, she'd deliberately resisted his at-tentions as long as possible to try to regain control over her life. But always, in the end, she had weakened.

One such memorable occasion had been last Sunday, soon after he'd had his private talk with his mother. She had thought when the two of them emerged smiling at each other that Uzziah had softened in his harsh intention of sending Irene on her way within half an hour. But he hadn't, it seemed. In no time, the helicopter took off for Casablanca, passenger and all. Beth had been shocked at this callous dismissal of his mother, and said so once they were alone in his quarters.

'She has a sizeable cheque for a new women's refuge,' was his sardonic reply. 'What more does she want?'

'What more does she want? My God, you're in-human, do you know that? She's your mother. She loves you. The women's refuge was clearly just an excuse to come here and make up with you.'

'So she said.'

'And you don't believe her?'

His dark eyes flashed. 'It's hard to wipe away over thirty years' behaviour with a few belated con-fessions. She's still basically the same woman she was when she arrived. Have you forgotten what she called you?'

'Of course I haven't forgotten. But I can under-stand her thinking what she did. She's a woman of intense religious belief. She came here on a mission of Christian mercy, only to find you with what looked to be another of your never-ending succession of sex-mad bimbos. How did you expect her to think of me?'

Uzziah rounded on her. 'Sex-mad bimbos! I'll have you know that the women I go to bed with are all——'

'Yes, I know,' she cut in caustically. 'They are all genuine, loving, caring, wonderful women, I'm sure.'

He glared at her. 'Maybe not, but they sure as hell aren't bimbos! They're usually wealthy women in their own right, the daughters of millionaires, damn it!'

Beth's jealousy sent her temper flaring out of control. 'OK, so they're not bimbos,' she bit out. 'They're gorgeous, sexy, rich bitches who, believe me, look upon you as no more than a kinky diversion. I

can just imagine what they say afterwards. Guess who
I had this weekend? Uzziah, the stud! Oh, yes, he's
just as good as they say. A veritable hunk! A real
stallion! A——'

'Enough!' Uzziah roared, fists clenched, black eyes
blazing.

Beth's blue eyes were doing a bit of blazing of their
own. But it was herself she was most angry with. Not
him. Hadn't she warned herself not to fall in love with
him? Much as she might now understand what made
him tick, any emotional involvement with such a man
was still to be avoided at all costs. But it was too late,
wasn't it? She already loved the bastard!

'If the cap fits, wear it, Uzziah,' she lashed out.
'Act like a shallow, brainless stud and you'll be treated
like one!'

His large hands darted out to haul her hard against
him. 'You will not speak to me like that!'

She wrenched out of his grasp, fearful that even a
violent embrace could weaken her determination to
speak her mind. 'Why not? It's true, isn't it? Just
look at the way you dress. Half the time you look
like an escapee from a Hollywood set of *Kismet*. How
could you expect any woman to take you seriously?'

'I don't *want* any woman to take me seriously,' he
returned with cold fury. 'Neither do I care what they
think of the way I look. I dress to please myself, in
clothes I find both serviceable and comfortable. If
what I wear has the added benefit of turning my
female guests on, then well and good. That is, after
all, why I bring them here. Why I brought *you* here,
my dear Beth. But it's *I* who decides whom I take to
bed, not the other way around. I am no woman's

plaything, believe me. *I* make the rules and *I* play the shots. And don't you forget it!'

His hand snaked out to encircle her waist and draw her back very close, his other hand lifting to caress her throat in a gesture that could have been threatening, but wasn't. Instead, it was incredibly sensual, firm fingertips collaring her neck, then dipping down into the deeply slitted neckline.

When Beth gasped her response, his black eyes narrowed with an answering passion. His hands slipped inside the robe to caress her bare breasts, their rock-hard peaks telling him all he needed to know.

'You have no conscience,' she moaned.

'I do not find making love a matter of conscience,' he ground out, then began dragging the black robe quite roughly down over her bare shoulders. Beth knew that within seconds he would have her naked on the divan behind them and, while the mental image of what he might do then sent her pulse racing wildly, one last burst of pride demanded she stop him.

'No, don't!' she cried, shaking hands reefing the gown out of his and back up to her neck. She took a couple of steps backwards on jelly legs, all the while doing her best to look both reproachful and affronted.

'For heaven's sake, Uzziah! Maybe your mother goes too far in her strait-laced attitude to sex, but you go to the other extreme. You say you are no woman's plaything. Well, neither do I want to be treated as *your* plaything. I demand more respect than that. I am not a toy. I am a human being with feelings. What you wanted now was not making love, it was nothing more than raw sex!

'Last night was very special to me, Uzziah,' she went on huskily. 'Don't spoil it by turning what we shared into something cheap and vulgar.'

His scowl was black with frustration. 'I do not like being made to feel guilty over what I consider perfectly natural urges. There is no set time or place for a man and woman to make love. Neither is it ever cheap or vulgar!'

'*Making love* might not be, Uzziah,' she countered with a lump in her throat. 'But just having sex can be. I know...'

'You are thinking of your experience with that bastard again. It has warped your mind.'

'All human beings have experiences that warp their minds to some degree,' she returned pointedly.

He grimaced, then heaved a ragged sigh. 'You could be right. Yes... you could be right. Look, I will write to my mother, see if we can't put our relationship to rights. Would that please you?'

Her heart lightened. 'Very much so.'

A devilish gleam sparked in his eyes when he saw her pleasure. Coming forwards, he drew her confidently back into his arms. 'Enough for me to claim a reward?'

Beth gasped as he bent to kiss her throat with soft, seductive lips. Quite automatically, her head tipped back, and she trembled. 'It's not Omar who's devious to the core,' she groaned. 'It's you.'

His head lifted, his eyes searching hers. 'Then you'll let me make love to you? Here, on the divan?'

'Would you really take no for an answer?'

'Probably not.'

'That's what I thought. You're still a barbarian, through and through...'

His mouth had been laughing as it claimed hers.

Beth remembered it well, as she remembered all her other subsequent surrenders. She really should never have stayed. The wrench to her heart was going to be terrible by the time she left the following Monday.

Sighing, she stood up and left the room.

'Did you get through?' Uzziah asked when she found him outside Amir's stable door.

She nodded.

His dark eyes searched her face. 'You've been crying. Is anything wrong back in Australia?'

Beth swallowed. 'No, I . . . I guess talking to Pete made me a little homesick.'

Uzziah nodded slowly. 'I can understand that. When I was in boarding-school I longed for the desert sands.' He reached out to cup her face, giving her such a sweet, gentle kiss that Beth almost burst into tears again.

'I will make you forget home,' he whispered against her lips, and began to draw her towards a nearby empty stable, his intention all too clear when his hands dropped to her buttocks.

She pulled away, angry with him, and herself. Already she wanted to give in. *Already*! 'Not *here*, Uzziah. Anyone could come along at any moment. Besides, you promised me that we would go riding together this morning.'

His scowl became a wry smile. 'You like to tease me, to make me wait. You really wish to go riding? Well, I suppose Flashy will accommodate you, now that she has had her wicked way with Amir.' He turned to pat the bay stallion's neck. 'But I think you will have to stay in here, my boy. That mare does not know how to behave around you.'

'You never did tell me the full story about Flashy and Amir,' Beth remarked while they waited for their mounts to be saddled, happy to find a distraction from her inner turmoil.

Uzziah sighed. 'She's always been a problem, that mare. God knows why I bought her in the first place.'

'Why did you?'

'It was one of those things. I was in England, over-seeing the delivery of a couple of my horses to their new owner when he persuaded me to join him at some local bloodstock yearling sales. Flashy took my eye straight away. She was so beautiful to look at and very spirited. Before I knew it she was knocked down to me. I sent her to one of the best trainers in England and, as you know, she won some very good races. But she was always breaking down. Finally, the vets advised she be put to stud.'

'And you had Amir cover her?'

'Good lord, no! I had her sent to the very best thoroughbred stallion in England, but she would have none of him, becoming quite vicious whenever they brought him near her. Even when she was secured and forcibly mated she failed to conceive. After a similar fiasco with a couple of other stallions the next year, I had her sent home here to me, with the intention of resting her, then having her put back into training. But she took one look at Amir and fell in love, if that's possible for a horse. Kicked a great hole out of her stable and jumped a never-ending series of fences to get at him. You rode the result in Egypt.'

'And has she had any other offspring to Amir?' Beth asked, thinking that the story was romantic and charming.

'Not as yet. Once it was confirmed she was in foal for the first time I shipped her back to England. After the colt was born and weaned she was put back into training. She won more races, but she pined for Amir, it seemed. She stopped wanting to race. So in the end I relented and had her brought home here, thinking I might let her mate with him again. Till I saw the disgraceful display that colt put on in Egypt! I do not breed undisciplined rogues. But it appears I do not have any say. Flashy has exerted her will again, as so many temperamental females do.'

'Is that so?' Beth stood with her hands on her hips, defying Uzziah with her stance and upturned nose.

His eyes narrowed as they raked over her. 'Yes, that's so,' he said in that quiet voice which bespoke the most danger. 'But sometimes, females meet a male whose will is stronger than theirs. Now mount up, woman. After our ride, I am going to show you the tower.'

'The tower? What tower?'

'Must you always ask questions? Just do as I say for once without argument.'

She smiled at him as she swung her tall body up into the saddle, smiled till he shook his head and smiled back. Slowly, their smiles became grins. They were both laughing by the time they rode off, the young Moroccan groom staring after them with a bemused expression on his face.

They rode for an hour, then returned to the castle to shower and change and have some lunch before Uzziah made good his promise of showing her the tower he had mentioned earlier, leading her through a maze of internal corridors then up a steep, winding staircase to emerge on the battlements that lined the seaward side of the citadel-like fortress.

For a moment, Beth was distracted by the freshness of the breeze and the sight of the ocean, which was being whipped up by the afternoon westerlies. Waves, huge and grey and threatening, crashed against the base of the cliffs down below, spewing foam and salty spray high up into the air, though not high enough to reach where they were standing.

Beth shivered, then glanced over at Uzziah, who was standing there, watching her closely. 'Aren't you cold?' she asked.

He was wearing the black silk pantaloons and black leather bolero he'd worn the first day she'd arrived, though without any cummerbund this time. Not that this was any concession to her earlier criticism over his exotic taste in clothes. He continued to dress in exactly the same fashion as before. And still to good effect.

Right now, she was finding it hard to keep her eyes from the expanse of bronzed, muscular flesh the skimpy bolero left uncovered.

'No, I'm not at all cold,' he answered, amusement in his voice. 'Come, I brought you here to look at the tower, not the ocean.' So saying, he took her elbow and shepherded her on up some more steps and around a corner.

'Well, what do you think of it?' Uzziah presented with an upward flourish of his left arm. His right was firmly around Beth's waist.

Her neck craned back.

It reminded her of how she'd imagined Rapunzel's tower as a child. Tall and narrow with a pointed spire and dark rectangular slits of windows, through which Rapunzel leant to let down her hair.

'It's like something out of a fairy-tale.'

'You think so?' Uzziah slanted a smile down at her. 'Would you like to go up there? The view is second to none.'

'I might get vertigo. I'm not all that good with heights.'

He pulled her close to his side. 'You don't have to worry. I won't let you fall.'

A heavy wooden door at the base of the tower led to an internal spiral staircase. They eventually emerged through a trapdoor into an empty, circular room with a wooden floor.

'It was a pirate look-out,' Uzziah explained as Beth gazed at the spectacular panorama through one of the windows, which were not as narrow as she'd thought from down below. 'If any of the men on look-out fell asleep on the job, they were thrown over the cliffs down on to the rocks below.'

Beth stared over at him, thinking to herself that he wouldn't have been out of place in those times. He was as ruthless and wild as that rogue pirate who had first lived here. Why, he even *looked* like a pirate. And yet, she had fallen in love with him. Madly. Irrevocably.

She shuddered and turned away, leaning against one of the high stone window-sills with clenched fists. Whatever was going to become of her?

Her heart started to thud when she felt Uzziah close up behind her. He lifted her long fair hair away from her neck, bending to kiss the pulse at the base of her throat. 'You are not as tough as you make out, are you?' he murmured. 'Inside, you are all warm and soft. All woman...'

Her stomach began to churn when she felt his arousal brushing against her.

'No one will come up here,' he went on in a husky voice, deft fingers undoing the buttons on her blouse, freeing her braless breasts to the play of his hands. 'We are as alone as we would be in my bedroom.'

Beth stiffened, well aware what he was asking of her. Once again, she rebelled against the idea of being so readily at his disposal. But as he caressed her breasts, pressing his need into the soft swell of her buttocks, a feeling of great love washed through her.

Just this once, she thought, I will show my love for him. I will not wait to be persuaded. Or seduced. I will give of myself freely, without reluctance, without inhibition.

With a soft moan of surrender she turned in his arms, lifting her hands to cradle his face and bring his mouth down hard on to hers. She matched him, kiss for kiss, touch for touch, caress for caress, undressing him and herself with trembling hands till they were both naked on the floor together.

For a long moment, he stared at her with a dark puzzlement in his eyes, but then she was urging him into her eager flesh, making him forget everything but the pleasure to be found in her woman's body. Beth listened to his breath catch, watched him close his eyes, then she, too, closed hers, her heart and body quickly soaring with his into a world of tempestuous excitement, a world that made one forget crippling things like a futile love. At least for a little while...

Afterwards she held him close, pretending for the moment that he did care about her, that he wouldn't be able to forget her in a hurry.

But he *would* forget her, Beth knew.

It might take a week, or a month, or even a year. But he would forget. Eventually. Hadn't he always?

'Must you leave tomorrow?' Uzziah asked testily.

Beth's chest contracted, but her expression remained steady. 'I have already stayed much longer than I originally intended, Uzziah. Very pleasant though my stay here has been, I have responsibilities that cannot be ignored.'

He said nothing, but she had the feeling that her reply annoyed him. Was it the lukewarm word 'pleasant' that he found offensive? Or the fact that a woman was refusing to fall in with his wishes? Surely it couldn't be that his emotions were engaged for once?

If you care for me at all, she thought desperately, then say so now, for pity's sake. Don't let me go like this. *Make* me stay!

But he remained silent.

They were standing at a fence, watching the foal that had almost died. It was still a touch on the small side, but getting stronger every day, so much so that Uzziah had moved it and its mother that morning into a stable that had a small yard attached.

'Beth,' he began abruptly.

Hope surged into her soul. 'Yes?'

He turned to face her. 'I want you to have the mare. Flashy. As a gift...'

Beth's heart sank. A week ago she would have snapped up the offer. But not now...now it would mean she was somehow putting a price on her love for Uzziah. Besides, the last thing she wanted was a constant reminder of him. Which was what Flashy would be. More than any other horse. For Beth was like the stubborn mare. There would only ever be one mate for her. No other would do but Uzziah. Of that she was certain.

She cleared her throat. 'Thank you, but no, I can't accept.'

'Why not?' he said sharply. 'You think it's some form of pay-off? If it makes you feel better you can give me some money for her, as much as you were going to pay for that stallion you wanted. She is far more valuable and is certain to be in foal to Amir again. She will probably have another black colt like the one you so admired.'

'No. Thank you again, but I have decided to buy an Australian horse, after all,' she lied bravely.

'You are a stubborn woman.'

'Yes,' she agreed.

'You really won't take the horse?'

'No.'

'Nor stay a while longer?'

'No.'

His stare became a glare. 'I will not beg you.'

'I don't expect you to.'

'I won't run after you.'

'Of course not.'

He scowled for a moment before speaking once again. 'Sometimes I do not think I like you, Beth Carney from Australia.'

'*Et tu, Brute*?' But that's because I love you instead, she flung at him silently.

He glared at her some more. 'We have only one day left, then?'

'So it seems.'

'We should not waste it arguing.'

'I couldn't agree more.'

He pulled her into his arms. 'You try my patience.'

'I don't mean to,' she choked out, a lump forming in her throat as the awful reality of the morrow finally hit.

'Beth, I——'

'Don't say anything more,' she rasped, her heart turning over. 'We have so little time. Just kiss me, Uzziah. Kiss me...'

CHAPTER FOURTEEN

THE helicopter hovered over the cobble-stones for a few brief seconds before rising swiftly upwards into the clear blue sky. Once above the domed roofs, it scooped down across the battlements and out to sea.

Beth leant her tear-stained face against the window, staring back at the cliffs and the castle above them, her eyes inevitably drawn to the tower where she and Uzziah had made such passionate love together.

Her stomach turned over.

'Oh, Uzziah,' she whispered against the glass. 'My love...my darling...'

As more tears started to roll down Beth's cheeks, a flash of red at one of the tower windows made her heart jump. Uzziah had been wearing a scarlet shirt that morning at breakfast...

He'd refused to see her off personally, saying he had said his goodbyes to her the night before. He also refused to go for one last early-morning ride with her—as had been their habit every day—claiming he had work to do after breakfast.

'I have been neglecting my duties while you've been here,' was his semi-reproachful remark over croissants and coffee. 'It is time for things to get back to normal. Your helicopter leaves in just over an hour. Please be ready. Omar must make a connecting flight to London.'

'Won't I...see you again?' Beth asked, an awfully large lump in her throat.

'No,' he pronounced abruptly.

'But——'

'Just go,' he'd snapped.

Terribly hurt by this curt dismissal, Beth had almost run to her quarters, where she found that Aisha had already packed her things for her. The girl was just closing the luggage when Beth rushed into the room. The two women's eyes met, Beth's still shimmering from unshed tears, Aisha's showing a tender sympathy that was very touching.

Beth closed the door and walked slowly over to the side of the bed. 'Thank you for packing for me, Aisha. You've looked after me as if I were a baby while I've been here. I'll miss you.'

'And we will *all* miss you, *mademoiselle*,' the girl insisted with a catch in her voice.

Beth then did something she had never done to another woman. She drew Aisha into her arms and gave her a long, hard hug. 'Thank you,' she choked out.

'Oh, *mademoiselle* . . .'

Beth drew back, shaken by the emotion that was crashing through her. 'Please don't cry. If you do I will surely break down. And I mustn't do that. I mustn't! I knew when I stayed on that Uzziah did not love me, that I would eventually have to leave.

'But I do not regret this time I have spent with him,' she went on sincerely. 'It has been . . . a wonderful experience, and one I will treasure for the rest of my life. So please . . . do not be sad for me. I want you to be happy, to have a happy life with Omar and your baby. Will you do that for me?'

The girl tried to smile through her tears. '*Oui, mademoiselle*, but . . . but I am not so sure that Sidi

Uzziah does not love you. He...he has been *different* with you than with any other woman.'

'Maybe, Aisha,' Beth murmured. 'But not different enough, I'm afraid. He still wants me to go. He said so.'

Aisha shook her head. 'But a man does not always say what is in his heart, *mademoiselle*, especially a man who has grown used to his own selfish ways. Sometimes he needs...how you say...a leetle push.' And she held a hand over her stomach.

Beth sighed. 'Somehow I can't see Uzziah responding to even a *little* push. He is very much the master of his own destiny.'

'Maybe, but...'

'No more, please, Aisha. If Uzziah felt anything special for me at all he would come to see me off, but he refuses. He did not even kiss me goodbye. I do not want to speak of him any more.'

But he *did* come to see me off, Beth realised as she stared at the fast disappearing tower and that flash of red. He *did*!

Her head whirled with a host of wildly exciting thoughts. What if Uzziah *did* love her? What if his brusqueness this morning was the result of his *own* distress, not indifference to hers? What if this unexpected love, this alien emotion, had made him act cruelly this morning out of a long-ingrained defensiveness?

After what Irene had told her, Beth could well understand why Uzziah kept himself distant from loving too much. For loving could be a very painful process indeed.

'Miss Carney...'

Beth jumped in her seat. She had forgotten that Omar was sitting right next to her.

'Yes?'

'I . . . I wish to apologise to you . . .'

She was startled. 'What about?'

'When I invited you here for my master, I thought . . . I assumed . . .' He shrugged. 'I was wrong about you,' he said simply. 'You are by far the nicest lady to have ever graced my master's home. I . . . I hope you will return some day.'

Beth's heart was filled to overflowing by Omar's generous compliment. 'And I was wrong about you, Omar,' she returned.

He blinked his astonishment.

'I thought you were terribly pompous,' she stated truthfully.

'And now, Miss Carney?'

She grinned at him. 'Now, I think you are only marginally pompous.'

For a second, he looked taken aback, then he grinned back at her.

'Tell me, Omar,' she went on, determined to take advantage of this new rapport between them. 'If Uzziah is so much against marriage then why did he insist on you and Aisha getting married? Now don't look so surprised. I know all about the baby and everything. Aisha and I are bosom buddies.'

Omar's expression was faintly appalled till he pulled himself together. 'I see . . . well, Miss Carney, the fact of the matter is that my master——'

'Oh, do call him Uzziah,' Beth broke in impatiently. 'I just can't abide that master business any longer!'

Omar's servile façade cracked appreciably at this. He even laughed. 'I can see why you have been such a success with Uzziah. But he is not against marriage. Wherever did you get that idea?'

'Aisha said as much.'

'Aah, I see. Well, perhaps that was the case with the sort of—er—ladies he has entertained here in the past. Some of them were quite forward in their ambitions to become mistress of the house, so Uzziah used to make loud noises about his aversion to marriage. But, in truth, he has nothing but respect for the institution. If his mother and father had been married, his life would have been considerably easier.

'Uzziah's one true aversion is to people who inflict their ideas and opinions on others, whether they be religious or political. His *domaine* here has become renowned in Morocco as a type of haven where people can come who've suffered at the hands of the rigid beliefs of others. Anyone who comes to work and live here is told quite firmly that, while they have the right to live their own personal lives by any rules they see fit, they must not hurt others, nor try to impose their own convictions on anyone else.'

'Is that what that young man had done?' Beth asked. 'You know, the one in the people's court, the one Uzziah became really angry with.'

'Ah, yes ... Mahmoud. He's been working in the vineyard, tending grapes, but did not approve of our making wine. His complaint was that alcohol was against his religion and he did not want to contribute to sinful practices. Uzziah quickly pointed out that alcohol wasn't against *his* religion, however. He also told the lad that there was no room in his *domaine* for such intolerance and bigotry. Faced with exile,

Mahmoud soon saw the light. All the workers here know there is no better man in Morocco to work for than Uzziah.'

'He is certainly very well respected,' Beth murmured.

'*And* loved.'

'Yes,' she agreed.

There was a short, sharp silence before Omar spoke again. 'Have you told him of your love?' he asked softly.

Beth shook her head.

'A pity, perhaps,' was all Omar said before they both lapsed into silence again. Neither of them said another word till the helicopter was coming in to land at Casablanca airport, whereupon Beth suddenly swivelled in her seat to face Omar, an expression of simmering excitement on her face.

'Omar! When will this helicopter be going back?'

'As soon as the week's supplies are loaded on. Why?'

'Can I go back with it?'

His eyes widened. 'I don't see why not.'

'Thank God.'

'Are you sure you know what you're doing, Miss Carney?'

'No, but I'm going to do it anyway. I have to find out Uzziah's true feelings for me, one way or the other. I can't just fly off into the sunset, always wondering if I'd thrown away my only chance for happiness with a man. I'll go mad if I do. I *have* to go back!'

Uzziah wasn't in the castle when she returned. He was out riding, Aisha told her.

Beth changed into jeans and a white shirt, then raced down to the stables and saddled Flashy herself. That was much easier than trying to explain to the stable-hands what she wanted, since they didn't speak much English. Only Uzziah's house staff spoke good English. But she did manage to find out the general direction in which Uzziah had gone.

Spurring Flashy into a fast gallop, she set off towards the mountains, following the path along the river before crossing a rickety wooden bridge and surging up a long, grassy slope. Reining in on the top of the first knoll, she searched the horizon for a sign of Uzziah and his grey gelding.

'There!' she shouted aloud, spotting his red shirt on a distant hill.

Presumably he must have seen her coming, for he stayed put till the spirited black mare carried Beth right up to where he sat waiting, an amazed look on his face.

'What in God's name are you doing back here?' he grated out.

'I had to come back,' she blurted out. 'I have something to say to you that has to be said.'

He simply stared at her, black eyes narrowed, his back tensely straight in the saddle.

She stared back, thinking that he had never looked more handsome, nor more frighteningly aloof than at that moment. Swallowing, she decided there was no other way than to simply plunge in before her courage failed her completely.

'I love you,' she stated bravely and boldly, though her voice was shaking. 'I know that you do not want any woman to love you, but I'm afraid there's nothing you can do about it, because I've gone and done it.'

'Is that so?' he replied in a tone that could have been dry if it hadn't been so thick.

'Yes, that's so! And you know what? I think you'll like the idea once you get used to it. I think you're sick to death of having a never-ending stream of women trail through your bedroom. You're ready for one woman, Uzziah. You're ready for some type of permanency. Perhaps not marriage yet. That's probably too big and too sudden a change for a man who's spent his whole life running away from getting too close to anyone because he thinks that can only bring pain. Oh, don't look so surprised, I know all about you and your past. Your mother told me!'

She saw him open his mouth to say something, but she raced on before he could get a word out. 'But there are other types of pain too, Uzziah, than the pain of rejection or even death. And the worst of these is loneliness. You're not getting any younger, you know. One day you won't look the way you do now. You won't pull the women in so easily. You'll end up a lonely, cynical old man with no children, no wife, no nothing!'

She scooped in a quick breath and kept going. 'But I'm not going to let that happen to the man I love because I'm going to keep coming back, Uzziah, till you find you cannot live without me. I have fifty thousand dollars still in my bank, which is a hell of a lot of plane fares to Morocco. Yes, I'm going to come back to you and your bed over and over, and one day, God help me, I'm going to have your child, and then, Uzziah, then you're not going to be able to turn your back on me so easily. You're going to look at me and want my love, *want* your child. You're going to want them both as desperately as I want *you!*'

Beth was unaware that by this time tears were streaming down her face. All she could see was Uzziah's eyes, his beautiful dark eyes, staring at her as though she had gone mad.

The silence was electric, punctuated only by Flashy's impatient snorting. As though in slow motion, Uzziah urged his horse forwards, closing the gap between them, bringing the grey gelding round till it was parallel with the black mare. His black gaze bored down into hers, making her heart pound with a terrified anticipation.

'Have you finished?' he ground out.

'Y...yes,' she said with sudden meekness. It was as though, now that her outburst was finished, all her strength and courage was draining away.

'Good. Because now I have something to say to you.'

'W...what?'

'You're absolutely correct.'

She blinked.

'I knew it as I watched that helicopter carrying you away. I knew it here...' He tapped the side of his head. 'And here...' He bluntly indicated his crotch. 'But mostly here...' He placed a solemn hand over his heart.

She blinked again, hardly daring to believe what he was telling her.

'I have never felt such heartache,' continued his amazing confession. 'The thought that I would never see you again, never hold you in my arms again, never be able to tell you what you mean to me...'

He snaked a hand around her neck and pulled her mouth to his in a long, torrid kiss.

'I love you, Beth,' Uzziah whispered into her swollen lips. 'The moment that helicopter disappeared from view I vowed I would come after you and bring you back. I came out here riding to plan my course of action.'

'Which was?' she asked dazedly.

'I was going to follow you to Australia and shamelessly seduce you till you couldn't live without me!'

'You *were*?'

'I thought your feelings for me were mainly sexual. After all, you'd virtually accused me of being little more than a stud, so I naturally thought my sexual prowess was my chief attraction for you. So I was going to exploit that to get you where I wanted you.'

'Which was?'

'Pregnant.'

'*Pregnant!*'

'It occurred to me that if it worked for Aisha it would work for me.'

'Goodness!'

'If all else failed I might have been forced to kidnap you then keep you tied to my bed forever.'

'Mmmm. That idea's not half bad...'

'You should not say such things,' he groaned. 'They drive me wild!' And he kissed her again till they were forced apart by Flashy skittering around.

Uzziah scowled at the mare. 'That horse is an infernal nuisance!'

Beth laughed. 'She's just frisky. She needs more exercise.'

'Does she, now? Well, why don't you race me to the next hill, then?'

'And if I win?' she asked teasingly. 'What do I get?'

'If you win, I'll marry you.'

'And if I lose?'

Uzziah sighed with mock drama. 'Alas and alack, if you lose, then *you* have to marry *me*.'

'How can I lose? I'm on to a sure thing!'

Suddenly, Beth's face fell, that saying reminding her of Pete and her riding school back in Australia. She couldn't possibly abandon them, no matter how much she loved Uzziah. Oh, dear heaven, why hadn't she thought of that before? It was all so impossible!

Uzziah seemed to read her mind. 'Don't worry,' he reassured her gently, his hand reaching out to touch her cheek. 'We'll work something out. Maybe we can live in both countries. Or maybe we can bring Pete and your horses over here. Love always finds a way, my darling.'

Beth's heart turned over. Uzziah loved her, really, really loved her. Dear God, if she didn't do something quickly she was going to burst into tears.

'You won't *let* me win, will you?' she said, quickly changing the subject. 'The race to the next hill, that is.'

His expression showed that was a ridiculous suggestion. 'I can't imagine any man *letting* you do anything, Beth Carney. Now off we go!'

The grey horse was away first, the black in hot pursuit. They flashed down the hill and across the valley floor, quickly neck and neck, manes and tails flying. But the black mare was much too fast, much too strong. She surged ahead, her rider exultant as she reached the crest of the hill with several lengths to spare.

'I won, I won!' Beth cried in happy triumph, fair hair flying out behind her, white teeth laughing, blue eyes sparkling.

Uzziah reined the grey gelding in beside her, his black eyes afire with love as they beheld his vibrant bride-to-be. 'Yes, my darling,' he said with passionate possession in his voice. '*You* won. But *I* got the prize!'

HARLEQUIN  PRESENTS®

The Heat is On!

Watch out for stories that will
get your temperature rising....

They're

Coming next month:

Savage Destiny by Amanda Browning

Harlequin Presents #1724

Was he just using her?
Five years ago, Pierce had married Alix one day—
and rejected her the next. Once was enough for
Alix—she'd been burned. But then came a new dilemma....
She had to marry Pierce again for the sake of her family.
But this time she wouldn't suffer—even if Pierce was
still too hot to handle!

Available in February, wherever Harlequin books are sold.

THTH-1

Fifty red-blooded, white-hot, true-blue hunks
from every State in the Union!

Look for MEN MADE IN AMERICA! Written by some
of our most popular authors, these stories feature some
of the strongest, sexiest men, each from a different state
in the union!

Two titles available every month at your favorite
retail outlet.

In January, look for:

WITHIN REACH by Marilyn Pappano (New Mexico)
IN GOOD FAITH by Judith McWilliams (New York)

In February, look for:

THE SECURITY MAN by Dixie Browning
(North Carolina)
A CLASS ACT by Kathleen Eagle
(North Dakota)

You won't be able to resist MEN MADE IN AMERICA!

If you missed your state or would like to order any other states that have already been
published, send your name, address and zip or postal code, along with a check or
money order (please do not send cash) in the U.S. for $3.59 plus 75¢ postage and
handling for each book, and in Canada for $3.99 plus $1.00 postage and handling for
each book, payable to Harlequin Reader Service, to:

In the U.S.
3010 Walden Avenue
P.O. Box 1369
Buffalo, NY 14269-1369

In Canada
P.O. Box 609
Fort Erie, Ontario
L2A 5X3

Please specify book title(s) with your order.
Canadian residents add applicable federal and provincial taxes.

MEN195

HARLEQUIN PRESENTS®

We can't keep them to ourselves any longer!
Our new collection of intriguing and sensual stories!

Everyone Has Something To Hide

Something which, once discovered,
can dramatically alter lives.

Original Sin by Rosalie Ash
Harlequin Presents #1723

Guilty love?

When Christian Malraux told Emily, "You will be my sex
slave," she should have turned tail and run! But she hoped
that the power of her love would bring Christian into the
light again. Because there was a dark secret in Christian's
past, which had scarred his soul, as well as his face....

Available in February, wherever Harlequin books are sold.

SECRETS-1

HARLEQUIN®

PRESENTS Plus

It wasn't the best start to a working relationship:
Debra's private detective sister had asked her to spy on
Marsh Graham—Debra's new boss! But if Debra began
by believing Marsh had suspicious motives, she soon
realized that, when it came to her, Marsh had desires of
a more personal kind....

Was Denzil Black moving from woman to woman, seduc-
ing them, then leaving them drained and helpless? Clare
thought of Denzil as a vampire lover...so when she realized that she was next on his list of conquests, she resolved that *Denzil* would learn what it was to be a victim of love!

In Presents Plus, there's more to love....

Watch for:

A Matter of Trust by Penny Jordan
Harlequin Presents Plus #1719

and

Vampire Lover by Charlotte Lamb
Harlequin Presents Plus #1720

Harlequin Presents Plus
The best has just gotten better!

Available in February, wherever Harlequin books are sold.

PPLUS21

On the most romantic day of the year, capture the
thrill of falling in love all over again—with

Harlequin's

Bachelors

They're three sexy and *very single* men who run
very special personal ads to find the women of
their fantasies by Valentine's Day. These exciting,
passion-filled stories are written by bestselling
Harlequin authors.

Your Heart's Desire by Elise Title
Mr. Romance by Pamela Bauer
Sleepless in St. Louis by Tiffany White

Be sure not to miss Harlequin's Valentine Bachelors,
available in February wherever
Harlequin books are sold.

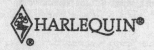

HARLEQUIN®

VB

HARLEQUIN®

Don't miss these Harlequin favorites by some of our most distinguished authors!
And now, you can receive a discount by ordering two or more titles!

HT#25577	WILD LIKE THE WIND by Janice Kaiser	$2.99 ☐
HT#25589	THE RETURN OF CAINE O'HALLORAN by JoAnn Ross	$2.99 ☐
HP#11626	THE SEDUCTION STAKES by Lindsay Armstrong	$2.99 ☐
HP#11647	GIVE A MAN A BAD NAME by Roberta Leigh	$2.99 ☐
HR#03293	THE MAN WHO CAME FOR CHRISTMAS by Bethany Campbell	$2.89 ☐
HR#03308	RELATIVE VALUES by Jessica Steele	$2.89 ☐
SR#70589	CANDY KISSES by Muriel Jensen	$3.50 ☐
SR#70598	WEDDING INVITATION by Marisa Carroll	$3.50 U.S. ☐ $3.99 CAN. ☐
HI#22230	CACHE POOR by Margaret St. George	$2.99 ☐
HAR#16515	NO ROOM AT THE INN by Linda Randall Wisdom	$3.50 ☐
HAR#16520	THE ADVENTURESS by M.J. Rodgers	$3.50 ☐
HS#28795	PIECES OF SKY by Marianne Willman	$3.99 ☐
HS#28824	A WARRIOR'S WAY by Margaret Moore	$3.99 U.S. ☐ $4.50 CAN. ☐

(limited quantities available on certain titles)

	AMOUNT	$
DEDUCT:	10% DISCOUNT FOR 2+ BOOKS	$
ADD:	POSTAGE & HANDLING	$
	($1.00 for one book, 50¢ for each additional)	
	APPLICABLE TAXES*	$_____
	TOTAL PAYABLE	$_____
	(check or money order—please do not send cash)	

To order, complete this form and send it, along with a check or money order for the total above, payable to Harlequin Books, to: **In the U.S.:** 3010 Walden Avenue, P.O. Box 9047, Buffalo, NY 14269-9047; **In Canada:** P.O. Box 613, Fort Erie, Ontario, L2A 5X3.

Name:_____

Address: _____ City:_____

State/Prov.:_____ Zip/Postal Code:_____

*New York residents remit applicable sales taxes.
Canadian residents remit applicable GST and provincial taxes.

HBACK-JM2